Date D...

JE 10 '69

JY 1...

POLICEMAN'S DREAD

POLICEMAN'S DREAD

BY

JOHN CREASEY

CHARLES SCRIBNER'S SONS
NEW YORK

I

LETTER

DETECTIVE CONSTABLE BIRWITZ, of the 31 Division of
the Metropolitan Police, Criminal Investigation Branch,
heard his wife humming as she started preparing breakfast, and heard the postman whistling as he approached
the front door. Birwitz was giving his shoes a final
polish, sitting on the arm of a chair so that he could
glance right, and see Meg; or left, and see the passage
which led to the front door. This was a bungalow on the
border of the Division; new and pleasant, if small.

A shadow appeared against the frosted glass panels
of the front door.

Meg called: "One egg or two, Witz?"

She twisted round and looked at him, and sight of her
seemed to hurt. She wasn't exactly a beauty, but there
wasn't a woman in the world with a more provocative
figure, and when she turned like that, jumper straining
against her breasts, she was magnificent. The early
sunlight, catching a corner of the kitchen window, shone
on her corn-coloured hair and turned it golden.

"Did you hear me?" she called.

The metallic sound of the letter-box being pushed
open came at the same time.

"I heard," said Birwitz. "Trying to starve me to
death?"

"Two eggs," said Meg, and turned back to the gas
stove. Even standing with her back to him, she was a
temptation. Those legs; those curves from her waist to
her hips, accentuated by the narrow scarlet tape of her
apron and the big bow in which she had tied it. One
loop of the bow fell exactly dead centre.

Letters appeared—one, two, three. Thank God there

5

was more than one, Birwitz thought. He finished polishing the right shoe, put it down, and went in his stockinged feet to the front door. He was a tall, solidly-built man, who moved a little clumsily whenever he moved slowly; dark-haired, with a rather sallow skin. He did not look quite English, certainly not Anglo-Saxon. He stooped down.

There was a small letter in a pale blue envelope, which would be for Meg; there was an unsealed one, probably a bill; and there was the letter he had feared. That was in a cheap manilla envelope, typewritten, ordinary looking; the postmark was *London, W.1.* He slid this into his pocket quickly, almost guiltily, and stood with the others in his hand. Judging from the sizzling on the stove, breakfast wouldn't be more than three or four minutes, but he had to see what this morning's letter said.

Why must it be this morning? He couldn't avoid the court, he had to give evidence. Most other mornings he would be able to take time off, to make sure—

He swung round. Meg was leaning sideways to get something, and stretching upwards, too. He clenched his teeth as he thrust open the door of the bedroom and went in.

The tapestry curtains were drawn back; the net curtains were good enough to give them what privacy they needed from the street. He was oblivious of the compact garden, the bungalow opposite, the milkman's van being drawn slowly along. He turned sideways to the window, ripped open the letter, and smoothed it out. It read:

> *SHE'LL BE OFF AGAIN THIS MORNING,*
> *THE WHORE.*
> *WHY DON'T YOU PUT A CHASTITY BELT*
> *ON HER?*
> *AND WHY DID YOU HAVE TO MARRY A*
> *SLUT?*

Birwitz drew in his breath very thinly, hissingly, stood still for a moment, then slowly crumpled the letter in his hand. He thrust it into his pocket. The rustling of the paper, the chink of coins, and the sizzle of the frying eggs and bacon merged together. Birwitz moistened his lips, then moved slowly. He caught a glimpse of himself in the centre of the three mirrors in the dressing-table, and did not like what he saw in his own eyes, or the way his lips were tightened at the corners. There were veins like whipcords purple in his neck.

She'll be off again this morning, the whore . . .

At ten o'clock, he was due in court to give evidence against a middle-aged woman accused of shop-lifting. The case might not be heard until twelve or even one o'clock, but it could be called first. There wasn't any way of finding out in advance, nor any way of persuading the magistrate's clerk to call it early. In any case, what time would Meg leave?

Friday, Friday, Friday. She always went shopping in Richmond Market on Friday; she said it saved ten shillings on the week's groceries and meats, and was well worth the bus ride.

"Witzy!" she called.

He didn't answer.

There were moments when he could not believe that he even suspected her, and when he thought he must be crazy to take the slightest notice of these letters; but there were other times when he felt that he had to know for certain. He had to watch and follow her. The disturbing truth was that he always lost her—she moved so quickly, and his time was so limited. He could not bring himself to pay someone else to spy on her, and if he asked anyone at the Station it would be like telling the world. Whatever was done, he had to do himself. He had to satisfy himself that the letters were false and vicious and that Meg was all that he believed her to be. The good things.

"Witzy! You'll be late."

She had a kind of lilt in her voice, a lilt which had first attracted him to her. She had come with a party to Imber Court, the Police Sports Ground, a guest of a policewoman. He had been looking for a game of tennis, they had drawn lots, he had drawn her as a partner.

"Your bad luck," she had said, in that attractive voice, and with a gleam in her blue eyes. She was the most perfectly-coloured Anglo-Saxon type anyone would ever see. Her cheek-bones were a little too prominent, her jaw a little bony, her eyes a little—just a little—sunken, but they were big, bright and blue. And that body! The difficulty had been to keep his eyes off her as she had run about the court. That was four years ago. They had been married for three and a half years. Until three months ago, when the first letter had come, he had thought himself the happiest man on the metropolitan force.

"*Your bad luck.*"

"Where the devil is that man?" Meg said in a clear voice, and he heard her slapping plates down on the table. Then she came along the passage, heelless slippers clack-clacking on the polished parquet floor. "*Witzy!* Your breakfast is getting cold and your Boss will be getting impatient. I—" She reached the doorway, saw him, and stopped. Alarm sprang into her eyes, driving momentary exasperation away. "*Darling!* What's the matter?"

Could anyone speak like that without being really concerned? Could such a *darling* be false?

"I—I've got a hell of a headache," Birwitz said.

"Another headache!"

"It's thumping."

"When did it start?"

"It—it wasn't too good when I woke up."

"You didn't say anything."

"I didn't—I didn't want to worry you."

"But you're having too many headaches," Meg protested. "Have you—?" She broke off, as if at some unpleasant thought, and then squared her shoulders. "Have you seen a doctor?"

"Doctor?"

"Yes, a doctor. One of those men with stethoscopes and blood pressure gauges and—" She stopped being semi-flippant, as if she realised that it was the wrong moment for flippancy, even to help hide her anxiety. She drew closer. "You look awful."

"I'll be all right."

"Can you stay at home this morning?"

Would she suggest that if she were anxious to go out?

"No, I—I'm due in court."

"They can get along without you for once."

"Not this time," he said. He was feeling better already, partly because she was standing so close to him and looking so concerned. Whenever she was close, it was better. He could half believe the hideous things about her when she wasn't with him, even when her back was turned, but to stand and look at her now made it impossible to believe them. The honesty in her eyes was like the purity of a blue sky. "I—I've got to give evidence of catching a woman shop-lifting."

"They could postpone the hearing."

"No," said Birwitz. "You know they can't. I'm feeling better already. I—probably I'm hungry." He felt ashamed, and yet knew that the moment he stepped out of the front door he would begin to doubt again. Doubt was like a cancer. But for the moment he felt almost normal. "What are you keeping me waiting for?"

Meg didn't answer back, but turned and led the way into the kitchen; it was almost as if she suspected that he had been lying. She had put their plates on the table, which was laid for breakfast with as much care as if important guests were staying; she was the most house-proud woman he knew, which probably went some way towards explaining her own rather scrubbed look. The chairs were drawn out from the table, and the coffee pot was on a small electric hotplate, the kind now used in restaurants. He waited until Meg sat down, then took his place. Two sausages, three slices of bacon, two eggs, two pieces of fried bread and a few pan-fried potatoes filled a dinner plate. He ought not to feel hungry, but he did. He glanced at Meg's plate; she was nearly as big an eater as he.

She was staring at him.

"Better?"

"Yes, much."

"What's the pain like, dear?"

"It's—it's a kind of pounding. When I bend down," Birwitz added, hurriedly; the lies never came easily, it had always been difficult to lie to Meg about anything. "Forget it."

"You must see a doctor."

"I'll fix it."

"I mean you *must*."

"I'll get Doc Aston to give me a onceover."

"When?"

"Some day soon."

"That's not good enough, Witz."

He made a face at her. "Forget it. It's probably a kind of migraine. Lofty Gedge gets them very badly. I've seen him looking as white as a sheet one minute, and . . ."

"You'd better eat," Meg said at last.

They were unusually quiet and sober during the meal. It was possible to imagine two reasons for Meg's manner. One, anxiety about him; two, a guilty conscience. What a bloody fool he was!

He finished eating, and Meg poured him a second cup of coffee. He stood up as soon as he'd finished it. She was looking up at him.

"I must be off," he said.

"You take it easy," Meg urged. She stood up, although she hadn't finished her meal, and went with him to the front door. He took a narrow-brimmed blue trilby off a peg behind the door, stuck it on at a rakish angle, and asked:

"How do I look?"

"All right." She was standing just in front of him, only at arm's length. The light was shining on her through the glass panels and the open door of the bedroom; it made a kind of beacon of her eyes.

"Meg," he said, chokily, and quite suddenly and violently he pulled her to him, crushing her close, feeling her sharp intake of breath, the soft cushion of her breasts. He felt as if he could squeeze and squeeze and squeeze. She was trying to hold her head away, but it was difficult. His mouth was close to hers. His voice was hoarse. "Meg, you do love me?"

"*Love* you," she echoed. It was like a sigh.

"Do you?"

"With everything," she said. "With everything. Witz, what—?"

He let her go.

"Must be off," he said. "Make a fool of myself if I stay here any longer." He squeezed her hands, and turned and fumbled with the catch at the door. "Bye, sweet."

"Witz—"

"Must go."

"Witz, what's the matter?"

"Damned headaches."

"Witz, answer me. What's the matter?"

"Overdoing it, I suppose," he said. "Can't a chap tell his wife how much she means to him? Rather than lose you, I'd—" He broke off, amazed at what he was starting to say. Could a man be a bigger fool? "I'll be back early with luck." He pulled the door wide open and stamped on to the tiny porch.

She didn't speak again, but when he reached the

gate she was still standing at the open door, biting her lower lip, frowning. Anxious or guilty? Even now that she was a few yards away from him he could feel the doubt seeping back. The absolute trust which he had once felt, and which he knew whenever he was holding her, was fading.

He waved, turned, and walked swiftly towards the corner of Hillrick Avenue. Some of the letters had told him that men called at the house, and stayed long enough to take her to bed; to *his* bed. If he watched, neighbours would know. All he could do was to question her obliquely, about tradesmen, canvassers, door-to-door salesmen—

He couldn't go on much longer without being sure, and there was just one man he could trust to watch Meg; an old friend and a man in the Force—Manny Thompson. It was a hideous thing to ask anyone to do, but he simply couldn't go on.

It was a ten minutes walk from the bungalow to the bus stop in Upper Richmond Road, twenty minutes from there to the police station where he was due this morning at nine-thirty. He had been late the night before, and so had a little dispensation this morning. He swung round the corner, and glanced back. Meg wasn't at the gate; she seldom was. He lengthened his stride. He was fit as well as long-legged, and used to enjoy the walk, but lately it had done nothing to help him.

He touched the letter in his pocket. If he never saw it again, he would remember the words to the day he died, and one word, *whore*, seemed to hover in front of his eyes now. *Whore*, and *slut*.

Who would use such words about his Meg? Who would use such words unless there was some justification for them? How did he know they weren't true? Could he beg off the court hearing? Dare he? One middle-aged woman, who would plead klepto-mania, would get off if he failed to turn up, that was

all. What harm would that do? He could plead illness.
He could pretend—

He reached the bus stop. He knew quite well that he
would go to the station, and then to court, and would
wait there until he had been called to give his evidence.
It was a disciplined compulsion which he could not
disobey. But on the way, at the office, in the witness
box, while one part of his mind would be going through
the motions, the other would be thinking of Meg,
whore, slut, bed, those damnable letters.

This morning's was the tenth.

2

WITNESS

BIRWITZ sensed the excitement the moment he entered
the C.I.D. office; it showed in the glint in Corby's eyes.
Corby was a detective sergeant who was only a few
months off retirement, and usually behaved as if every
crime under the sun was routine. The Superintendent's
door was closed, too; at this hour it was usually open,
and the old man could be heard booming his orders
for the day. Alderman, another detective constable,
tall, thin, bony, also had a look of eagerness.

"You would choose this morning to be late," Corby
grumbled.

"Who's late?" questioned Birwitz.

"Haven't you heard the big news?" demanded
Alderman.

Birwitz made the effort needed to put a word and
a picture of Meg out of his mind.

"No. What's it all about?"

"Manny Thompson saw a man breaking into one of
the Riverside Drive houses last night, and went after
him," Alderman burst out. "The swine shot him."

Birwitz felt a cold sense of shock and dismay.

"Is he hurt badly?"

"He'll live to get his George Medal," Corby put in sardonically.

"Now what's this?" demanded Birwitz. He was bemused and shaken, and there was the crash of disappointment because he had made up his mind to confide in Manny, so as to ease the gnawing tension. Somehow, he had to pass this off, had to cover the depth of his dismay. "Manny been making a hero of himself?"

"You can say that again," Alderman declared. "He went after the swine, in spite of a bullet in his shoulder, and held him until help arrived. The swine's up this morning, and West of the Yard is with the Old Man now, going over the details."

Birwitz said, "Big shot, eh?"

Relief that Thompson was not badly hurt was tainted by his personal disappointment, and by the fact that this happening made it almost certain that his own case would be late. All strings would be pulled to see that Chief Superintendent West was given priority, and anyhow a charge of wounding, possibly of attempted murder, would be heard before a humdrum charge against a shop-lifter.

Birwitz sensed that the others were looking at him curiously, as if his reaction was not what they expected; naturally they would expect him to show more excitement and concern for Manny Thompson. He tried to cast off the shadow of Meg and the letter, and asked brusquely:

"Manny in hospital?"

"Richmond Cottage Hospital," Alderman confirmed. "They say he'll be out in a few days."

"His mother been told?"

"Of course she has," said Corby, as if the question was absurd. Then a telephone bell rang, and he turned to answer it.

Alderman moved away from his desk, and said: "I'll be back in four shakes, Witz."

He went out, and the door swung slowly to. Corby talked on the telephone, obviously to a newspaperman. Birwitz went to his own desk.

This station was being modernised, but they hadn't got down to the C.I.D. room yet. There were six high desks with sloping tops, rather like big old-fashioned school desks, with a leather-topped stool in front of each. The desks were placed back to back in rows of three, and on a flat shelf which ran along the middle were the IN and PENDING trays. In PENDING were all the details covering the charge against that old bitch Haughton. Birwitz glanced through this, to refresh his memory on details, and Corby finished telephoning.

"Nothing but questions," he complained.

"Much else in this morning?" Birwitz asked. "For the Courts, I mean?"

"One child in need of care and attention, three speeding cases, a breaking and entry . . ."

Corby reported mechanically, the list growing bigger and bigger, and Birwitz gave up any hope of an early hearing for his case.

So he would have time on his hands, time to think— time to imagine what Meg might be doing.

* * * * *

The next room was nearly as large as the C.I.D. room, which held eight men, but was exclusive to Divisional Detective Superintendent Nunn. Nunn's office had doors leading to the C.I.D. room, and to the passage.

Chief Superintendent Roger West sat opposite Nunn, outwardly pleasant and unhurried, but feeling a little impatient because Nunn had to say everything at least twice. Nunn seldom had a case of this importance— attempted murder, against a well-known criminal—and was excited by it.

Roger West was chiefly interested because the investigation might have repercussions in the East End of London, where the accused lived, and where he had a lot of friends. Roger would get busy on that as soon as he returned to the Yard. Meanwhile he would attend the Court hearing here, hoping that the Press would make an even bigger splash of this story and put the prisoner's friends on edge.

It was simply a question of waiting for the hearing; Nunn had said he would make sure that the case was up by ten-thirty. Now he was saying that he hoped West would stay and have lunch.

"I don't think I should," Roger said. "They're keeping some jobs on ice for me." Out of the blue, he asked: "Any problems among your staff, Charlie?"

"Staff?" echoed Nunn. "C.I.D. you mean?"

"Mainly, yes."

"Don't think so," said Nunn. "This is only a little show, you know. I've got an Inspector, two sergeants and four detective constables. All the rest are uniformed men. The seven are pretty sound, I think. Why?"

Roger said: "We've had a few cases of attempted bribery lately."

"Oh, no fear of anything like that among my chaps," Nunn assured him, almost over-confidently. "Like to have a word with them?"

"Just in passing," West replied.

Corby was obviously an old trooper; Alderman created no particular impression. Birwitz was the only one of the three men on duty whom Roger found interesting. That was partly because he had heard of him as a tennis player for the Metropolitan Police, partly because he had a feeling that Birwitz was on edge. This was no more than an impression, and at first Roger gave it no serious thought. It was not until he was sitting in court, with Birwitz present for another case, that he noticed the way the man's big, strong hands were clenched, and the tension of his body.

Birwitz kept glancing at his watch, too, as if impatient for his case to be heard.

Hobber, the burglar who had shot the police constable, was in the dock at ten-thirty-five. He was nearly bald, and he needed a shave, although his facial hairs were little more than down. His mild appearance and husky voice made it almost impossible to believe that he had spent twelve of the last seventeen years in jail, and was known to be one of the most vicious criminals in London.

Nunn conducted the police case with heavy-mannered thoroughness.

". . . and on behalf of the police I ask for a remand in custody, your honour, in order that further inquiries can be made."

The Chairman of the magistrates was a massive man, who looked more qualified for the dock than the bench.

"But you are going to offer some evidence, Superintendent?"

"Of course, sir."

Birwitz was staring at the clock above the Chairman's head.

"Then proceed, please, proceed."

A youthful householder who had been aroused by the shooting, gave evidence first; the man in the dock was the man he had seen struggling with a wounded policeman. Corby gave evidence that fingerprints found on the handle of the gun coincided with those of the accused. The Chairman and his two colleagues, a man and a woman, went into an unnecessary huddle before the chairman announced the inevitable remand. The whole hearing was over in twelve minutes.

Roger watched the man Birwitz more closely, seeing that his tension was increasing, feeling more than ever sure that something was on this man's mind.

Three motoring offences were quickly judged, and fines imposed; then a messenger came for Birwitz. Roger stayed, to watch and listen when a well-dressed,

haughty middle-aged woman was brought into the
dock, and behaved as if this was not only a great
indignity but a grave injustice.

"I wish to state as I stated at the time that this is a
wicked mistake, and I had every intention of paying
for—"

"Later, madam, later." The Chairman had heard
this kind of protestation too often to be impressed. "Is
the accused represented?"

A fair-haired young man in a black coat and striped
grey trousers stood up at once.

"Yes, your honour, I represent Mrs. Haughton."

"Then be good enough to make her understand that
when the time comes for her to make a statement, I will
inform her. . . . Doubtless you have already made it
clear to her that the case may be dealt with here, or
may be sent to a higher court?"

"Yes, sir, I have. Mrs. Haughton is so convinced that
the evidence which will be placed before the court will
establish her innocence that she . . ."

Nunn had come to Roger's side.

"Dunno that I like this, Handsome," he remarked
in a whisper. "Thought it was all cut and dried."

"Birwitz sure of himself?"

"Absolutely," Nunn asserted. "Sound as a bell."

A saleswoman at a local departmental store gave
evidence that she had seen the accused with two pairs
of nylon stockings, one leather handbag and a quantity
of costume jewellery in her possession, none of it paid
for. As the store manager repeated the testimony, Roger
could understand Nunn's puzzlement, for this had
every indication of a clear-cut and all too familiar case.

The solicitor for the police called Birwitz. In the witness box, he stood straight, and seemed sure of himself.

". . . and were you in the shop at the time of the
offence?"

"Yes, I was—"

"Your honour," interposed the youthful solicitor,

"may I point out that no offence has yet been proved?"

"I know, I know," the Chairman said testily.

The solicitor for the police, a middle-aged man who should have known better, glanced round at West and Nunn, then turned back to the bench. Birwitz was standing rigidly in the box, and Roger thought: Why can't he relax? What's he afraid of?

"Were you in the shop at the time of the alleged offence?" asked the solicitor, carefully.

"Yes, sir."

"Did you see the accused take an unusual course?"

Birwitz said: "She picked up a number of articles, including stockings, a leather handbag and some costume jewellery, and put them in a bag which she was carrying."

"Did she show these articles to a sales assistant?"

"Not as far as I could see, sir."

"Will you tell the court what happened then?"

Birwitz showed his hands for a moment; they were clenched, the knuckles bulging. As he began to tell his story, of a kind which had been told a thousand times before, Roger wondered whether anyone else sensed the unusual tension in the atmosphere. He glanced at the two grey-haired and one boyish looking man in the Press box; they weren't as bored as the Press often was. The Chairman was frowning. Nunn sat stiff in his seat. Everyone familiar with this kind of procedure sensed a coming clash, of course; this wasn't going to be straightforward.

Birwitz finished his answer.

"Mr. Cartwright." The Chairman looked at the young solicitor for the accused.

"I would like to ask the witness one or two questions," Cartwright said. He had both poise and confidence, as if knowing exactly what he was about. "Detective Constable Birwitz, you have told the bench that you had been detailed to visit this particular store because shop-lifters appeared to have been busy there recently. Was there any specific reason for this, do you know?"

Birwitz said: "I was detailed to go."

"Yes, we know that. Was any specific reason given to you?"

"No."

"Are you sure?"

Birwitz seemed to stiffen to attention.

"Yes, I am sure."

"There's nothing you have forgotten?"

"Nothing at all."

"*What the hell's he driving at?*" Nunn whispered in Roger's ear.

"You weren't told to look out for any particular person, then?" said the solicitor. "Your senior officer didn't say: 'That old bitch Mrs. So-and-So has been up to her tricks again at Witt's Stores. Go and see if you can catch her red-handed.'"

The woman on the bench looked down her nose. Mrs. Haughton glared.

"I was not," said Birwitz.

"When you reached the store, did you speak to anyone before mixing with the customers?"

"Yes."

"With whom did you speak?"

"The manager."

"Please be more specific. There are departmental managers, floor managers and general managers, aren't there?"

"I spoke to Mr. Entwistle, the general manager."

"Who began the conversation?"

Birwitz hesitated. The reporters were very intent, Nunn obviously didn't like the situation at all, but Roger's chief interest was still in the witness. Birwitz wasn't relishing the situation, but many a young detective disliked his early cross-examination. This wasn't simply a matter of being put off-balance, or of being bewildered. It went deeper.

"Don't you remember, Mr Birwitz?"

"I remember perfectly."

"Then who began the conversation?"

"Mr. Entwistle."

"What did he say to you?"

"He told me that he had reason to believe that some shop-lifters were active in the store and asked me to keep my eyes open."

"Did he indicate any of the suspects?"

Birwitz hesitated, with very good reason. The implication was crystal clear; that he had been told in advance to watch Mrs. Haughton, and had been prejudiced against her from the beginning.

"Mr. Birwitz, don't tell the court you can't remember what happened that morning," the young solicitor said sardonically. "It was only yesterday, remember." When Birwitz didn't answer immediately, he went on sharply: "Can you remember what happened *this* morning?"

Birwitz said stiffly: "There is nothing wrong with my memory."

"Did Mr. Entwistle point out any particular person?"

Birwitz said: "He mentioned three, including Mrs. Haughton."

"Ah!" exclaimed the solicitor, as if with deep satisfaction. "Now we are getting somewhere. Will you tell us exactly . . . ?"

*   *   *   *   *

"We find some doubt in this case," declared the Chairman of the Magistrates, as if reluctantly. "It has been clearly established that some customers at this particular store did in fact serve themselves, in the modern manner and present the goods for payment afterwards. We do not think that the prosecution has proved that the accused had no intention of paying. Case dismissed."

"The damned old fool!" growled Nunn. "But I've

got to admit that the solicitor would have tied up a more experienced man than Birwitz. Surprised it shook Birwitz so badly, though. Notice how he went pale when he was accused of having a bad memory?"

"I noticed," Roger said. "What's he got on his mind?"

"Birwitz? Shouldn't think there's anything," Nunn declared. "He's got an attractive wife, nice home—very nice home in fact." Nunn broke off, looked at Roger uneasily, and went on: "He didn't give his evidence well, I agree. When a copper gives the impression that he's not sure of himself the Bench often goes against him. Like to have him in?"

"Shouldn't just yet," protested Roger. "Charlie, I daren't say this to half the Divisional Supers, but I know you're not stuffy. I'd like a chat with Birwitz, preferably at his house. Mind leaving it to me?"

"Being mighty secretive, aren't you?"

"Have to be on this job," Roger said, and Nunn gave him a long, deliberate stare, then shrugged his shoulders.

3

SENSE OF SMELL

BIRWITZ knew that he had shown up very badly in the witness box, and that he bore at least part of the responsibility for losing the case against Mrs. Haughton. He felt angry and resentful, not least because he could only blame himself. He also felt almost desperate, because while waiting for the case he had been haunted by that letter; and when the solicitor had challenged him to remember what had happened that particular morning, he could have screamed at the man. That had been the first clear indication of the state of his nerves.

He kept his self-control at the station, in spite of

being ribbed. A half-expected summons to the Old Man's office did not come, probably because the shooting of Manny Thompson was still the chief pre-occupation. Tommy was improving, but not yet allowed visitors.

It was a little after two o'clock when a call came in from the Yard, saying that a man who specialised in daylight house-breaking had been seen in the Division.

"Go and watch the Riverside Drive and the Avenue area," Nunn ordered. "The uniformed men will be on the look-out, too."

By two-thirty, Birwitz was passing the end of his own street. The temptation to look in on Meg was almost overwhelming, and he actually turned his motor-cycle towards the bungalow, then swung away, towards the large houses closer to the river. The truth had to be faced; he hated the idea of going to see Meg, catching her unawares, in case she did not want him.

In case there was someone with her.

"Don't be a crazy fool," he said savagely, and turned along another narrow but attractive tree-lined road. Each house and bungalow stood in its own grounds, each was well-tended, and early spring flowers were already making a splash of colour against the green.

He had to ride round three sides of a square to reach his bungalow, and stopped fifty yards away from it, then went on by foot. The sun came out from behind vast white, unnatural-looking clouds, and shone on the windows, which were as bright as mirrors, on the red tiles, the dull red brick walls, the deeper red of the paintwork, the trim squareness of the lawn, the im-maculate macadam path with white flints rolled in. Everything he possessed was in that bungalow; every-thing he loved.

A short, thin man, bareheaded, was walking along, carrying a narrow case of black plastic. He hesitated, and for a moment Birwitz thought: He's going to my

place. But the man hurried past, and Birwitz gave a
twisted smile at the realisation that for a moment he
had half-suspected *that* little slob—

A window at the front was open; so Meg was in.

He went into the front garden, walking briskly,
determined not to be furtive. Now that he was nearer
the bungalow, nearer Meg, he began to rail at himself
for having the slightest suspicion of her. He was smiling
and yet pent-up when he reached the back door. He
caught a glimpse of movement at the window, and
immediately there were hurried footsteps.

He opened the door, and Meg cried:

"Darling! How lovely to see you!" She was smiling,
hatless, breathless, and still wore her outdoor coat.
Obviously she was surprised, possibly she was confused. "Thank goodness I'm back." She held his hands.
"You'd never believe it, but I ran into Dorothy Melson
this morning and we had lunch at Bentall's. I haven't
been in long."

"Good job I didn't find you out," said Birwitz. He
returned the pressure of her hands, but let go quickly.
"I only looked in for a jiffy," he went on. "There've
been some prowlers about down by the river. The
uniformed chaps are out in strength."

"You've time for a cup of coffee," Meg said. "Sit
down for five minutes, precious."

Her manner was no different from usual, she sounded
as warm-hearted and eager as ever, but—*had* she been
out with an old school friend?

"Help me off with this," she said, and turned her
back on him and held her arms backwards, for him to
pull off her coat. It was an old habit now, but still
precious. In the days before their marriage, he would
pull the sleeves back and the coat off her shoulders,
then slide his arms round her and cup her breasts
firmly in his hands. The moment still held magic, but
almost for the first time he did not want to pull her
against him, or to touch her. Yet if he did not, she

would wonder why, and might start asking questions. He jerked the sleeves, held her for a moment, and pulled the coat off.

"Five minutes, you said."

"The kettle's on," Meg declared, and darted away, as if happily. She disappeared.

Birwitz stood holding the coat, a knobbly textured one of many colours, red, browns, greens, yellows. He heard the clatter of cups, and then became aware of something else; an odour of tobacco smoke. He and Meg were non-smokers; every penny they could spare went into this house. But most of the men at the station smoked, some heavily. Corby smoked a pipe, and the smell in his clothes was unmistakable.

Birwitz raised the coat to his face, and the odour became stronger. How could Meg's coat become impregnated with tobacco smoke in such a way? It was a pub smell or a smoking-room smell; not that from a popular restaurant. He put the coat into the hall wardrobe, now virtually certain that Meg had lied.

He would have to challenge her with it, but—not now. There wasn't time. Yet if he waited, if he started to drink coffee and talk, he would not be able to hold the questions back.

He slapped his cap on the back of his head, and raised his voice.

"Meg, I can't wait. There's a copper outside, calling me." He opened the front door and stepped out, then slammed the door. It seemed to cut off a surprised call from Meg.

He ran towards his motor-cycle; if she came to the window, she would see him, and believe his need for haste. He straddled the machine quickly, kicked the self-starter, and moved off. He couldn't resist a glance over his shoulder, and saw Meg by the open door. At that moment she looked hurtfully beautiful—as well as startled. He took a hand off the machine to give a casual wave, and went faster, hardly able to think.

Then, even above the roar of the engine, he heard a high pitched, quite unmistakable sound. A police whistle shrilling. He raised his head, concentrating, and slipped his gear into neutral. The alarm call came again, over on his left between him and the river; the quickest way was to turn left and left again. He roared along, passing two men who were standing and looking towards the river. Riverside Drive, where Hobber had been caught, was wide, with large houses on either side, and those on his right had lawns sweeping down to the Thames.

Outside the street gate of one house lay a policeman, body crumpled up, helmet lying yards away from his head. He wasn't moving. Birwitz swung his machine through the gateway, passed the fallen man, and saw that the front door was wide open. He acted almost without thought, jumping off his motor-cycle, resting it against the wooden porch pillars, glancing at the uniformed man, then along the road. The two men were running towards the scene, and a car engine sounded. Birwitz ran into the house. He heard nothing. He found himself in a square hall, beautifully furnished, with rooms leading right and left. A doorway on the left led to a large modern kitchen, and the back door was open. Birwitz raced out.

Lawns ran down to the placid river, weeping willows grew by the bank—and a man was climbing into a dinghy tied up to a new-looking landing stage. He was untying the painter and staring at the house. Birwitz felt a deep sense of satisfaction; the man hadn't a hope of getting away.

He was short and thickset, with a scared look on his face—but he hadn't been too scared to knock out the policeman. He got the dinghy loose but by then Birwitz was only twenty feet away. The man snatched up an oar, not to row with but to strike at Birwitz, who saw him raise it in both hands ready to bring it down on his, Birwitz's, head. Birwitz dodged to one side. The man put so much power into the blow that he lost his balance. Birwitz leaned over the edge of the jetty, grabbed his right arm, dragged him out of the boat, then pulled him towards the bank, his legs and feet gliding through the water. It was easy to hoist him up near the head of the jetty.

Pale grey eyes in a pale, round face were very close to Birwitz's.

"I'll come quietly," the man muttered. "I—I know when I'm beat." He was wet through as he stood in front of Birwitz, apparently scared by what he said.

Birwitz felt a sudden overpowering hatred for the man, worsened by his bitter, savage mood. He hit out, a powerful blow to the stomach, which brought the man's chin forward, then struck again and again. He saw blood. He saw the head drop out of sight. He heard someone shouting—and sanity crept back. He looked down at the creature at his feet, saw the lacerated lips, one badly swollen eye, the blood spattering shirt and collar.

Then a man arrived, breathless, gasping:

"You trying to kill him?"

Birwitz growled: "He tried to bash my head in."

"That doesn't give you—" the man began, then broke off as two uniformed policemen came hurrying.

The man on the grass did not move.

*　　*　　*　　*　　*

Birwitz stepped into Nunn's office at five o'clock that afternoon, tense and nervous, but no longer just because of Meg. Nunn was alone in the large, littered office. He looked his sixty years. His greying hair was very thin, and his face was lined. Usually, he looked a rather benevolent man, but now he was hard-faced, severe-looking.

"You sent for me, sir?"

"Yes, Birwitz." Nunn stared as if trying to see something he had not known existed. There was no

doubt of his sternness. "Have you heard of the condition of the man you assaulted this afternoon?"

"Assaulted isn't the word I would have used, sir."

"It's the word a lot of people will use," declared
Nunn. "The man is on the danger list at the hospital."

Birwitz thought: Oh, God, what have I done?

"I shouldn't have thought I'd hit him as hard as
that, sir."

"Well, you did."

"I suppose you have read my report, sir. He did
attack me with an oar."

"I've read your report, and I've read three eye-
witness accounts of what took place," said Nunn. "Two
were our men. The third was a local newspaperman
attracted by the whistle. All say the same. Up to the
time that you brought the man ashore, you behaved in
the best traditions of the Force. Afterwards you seem
to have taken leave of your senses. Was this man known
to you?"

"No, sir."

"Had you ever seen him before?"

"No, sir."

"Did you see his assault on Police Constable Smith?"

"I saw Smith lying unconscious," Birwitz said.
"How is he, sir?"

"Suffering from slight concussion, following a blow
on the back of the head against a corner of the wall,
when he was pushed off his balance. Birwitz, I want
you to tell me why you tried to kill the injured man."

"That's not true, sir."

"It's true in effect. But if you prefer it that way, what
made you attack this man so savagely?"

"He'd just attacked Smith, and tried to brain me."

"Were they the only reasons?"

"Yes, sir."

"I see," said Nunn. He paused, then went on
grimly: "When the reports of this affair reach the
newspapers, it will do the Force a grave disservice.

I trust you are aware of this. The reporter from the local paper sent a report to a national newspaper, and has described it as an attack of unbridled savagery on a defenceless man. There have been too many reports of police brutality lately, and this will be the worst case yet. Every policeman in England will suffer because of it. The respect of millions of people will be lost."

Birwitz didn't speak.

"Nothing to say?" barked Nunn.

Birwitz said: "I'm sorry you feel like that about it, sir. Obviously you've condemned me already, so there isn't much point in me saying anything."

"You don't think you stand self-condemned?"

"No, sir."

Nunn growled: "I don't know what's got into you. You were one of the most promising men here." He pushed his chair back and stood up, his fists clenching. "What's the matter, Birwitz? What's got into you? If you've got something on your mind, tell me about it. I might be able to help."

"There is nothing, sir."

"Very well," said Nunn, and his voice and manner became hard and formal. "You are suspended from duty till further notice. You will continue to draw your salary until such time as I have had contrary orders from New Scotland Yard. There will be a disciplinary inquiry, and you will be required to attend."

Birwitz thought wildly: The bloody fool, the silly bloody fool! The impulse to shout, the rush of blood to his head, the way his hands bunched, were all identical with his reactions when he had attacked the man in the boat. He saw a flare of alarm in Nunn's eyes—the Old Man's hand actually hovered over the bell-push. He didn't press.

"Do you understand, Birwitz?"

Birwitz said stonily: "Yes, sir." He thought: I'm

being kicked out. I'm being kicked out of the Force.

Nunn's fingers moved from the bell-push.

"All right. You can go."

Birwitz turned on his heel with military precision. On the way to the door, in just three strides, he began to hate the thought of facing the men in the other office, Corby and Alderman. He did not want to face anybody. He did not trust himself to keep his head. The crazy old bastard!

He swung away from the inner office door towards the passage, not caring what Nunn thought, pulled open the door and strode out. No one was in sight. His footsteps rang out on the hard composition flooring. He pushed open glass doors leading to the uniformed branch offices. A young constable coming out of a doorway stopped and gaped. Birwitz turned and half ran down the stairs. The charge-room sergeant was in his doorway, big and uniformed. "Good-eve—" he began, and broke off. Birwitz stormed past, down more steps and into the street. To the right was the yard and his motor-cycle. He turned left.

Two men, one old, one very young, seemed to appear out of the wall by his side.

"Mr Birwitz!"

"Detective Constable Birwitz, can you spare a moment? We represent the Allied News Agency, and—"

Birwitz glared, and pushed past them, lengthening his stride. He was tempted to break into a run, but restrained himself. *He'd been fired.* Nunn could call it suspension, call it what he liked, but this was the end of all his hopes, all his ambitions. *Fired.*

"There will be a disciplinary inquiry and you will be required to attend."

He turned a corner—and a car horn blared as he stepped blindly into the road. He crossed the road which led to the river, away from the High Street and the throngs of people. He kept walking, the hurt still raw.

It was not until half past six, when he reached the river at a spot where there were bungalows built like his, that he thought of Meg.

This was *her* fault.

4

FURY

Meg Birwitz thought: I wish he'd come now.

It was after nine o'clock, and the lights had been on for two hours. Usually she took such lateness for granted, sometimes hardly realising that it was dark, busying herself, reading, or looking at the television— although she preferred to be able to hear Witzy come in.

Tonight her mood was very different, because of what had happened this morning and this afternoon. She had never known him run off like that, and his manner had made her recollect other little signs that he hadn't been himself lately. She had noticed tensions in the past few weeks, and put them down to his almost obsessive application to his work. He slaved at it; sooner or later he would have to slow down. The peculiar thing was that he hadn't told her about Manny Thompson; she had heard about that on the radio.

Had that upset him?

To make the situation worse, he hadn't telephoned to say he would be late; she couldn't remember the last time he had failed to. She often teased him, saying that he was simply anxious to make sure supper wasn't spoiled.

Supper tonight was grilled sole, which wouldn't take long. She had a nibble at some biscuits and cheese, but was now feeling really hungry. She wanted to get supper. She longed to telephone the station, yet did not want Witz to think that she had been fussing. But at half past nine, she could stand it no longer, and went to the telephone.

"He went off duty about six o'clock," the Night Duty C.I.D. man told her. "Isn't he home yet?"

Meg said: "No. No, but it doesn't matter, I've just remembered—" She broke off, trying to find some excuse for having called, sensing that she must pretend that it wasn't really important. "—He was going to see a film on his way home, there's a horror thing I'd hate and he'd love!" She gave a rather high-pitched laugh; it sounded false even to her.

"That's all right then," the C.I.D. man replied. "Good-night, Mrs. Birwitz."

"Good-night."

She rang off, but did not move away from the telephone. Now she was frightened, although she could not have said why. Witzy's strangeness; the passion of his grip that morning; everything.

She closed her eyes and tried desperately to think of some explanation, something other than the obvious: that there was another woman. Have I been wrong? she asked herself fearfully. Should we have had children before we got everything for the home? That was a question she had begun to ask herself in the past few months, for her own sake. They had agreed to get the home paid for, to be out of debt, before starting a family. The question was more urgent now. Could there be another woman?

She went to the front door, opened it, shivered in a chill wind, but crossed her arms in front of her breasts, hugging herself, and walked quickly to the gate. A cyclist passed, coming away from the river, light wobbling. She looked along the dimly lighted street, seeing four other bungalows with bright lights shining from the windows, the others in darkness. A car passed the end of the road, but no one was walking, and there was no sign of a motor-cycle.

A gust of wind swept off the river, and made her shiver violently. She hurried back, closed the door, and was glad of the centrally-heated warmth of her home; but she was much more frightened now.

Manny Thompson, the one man to whom she could have talked, the one man in whom Witzy might have confided, was in hospital.

She went back to the kitchen, where the filleted fish was ready to go under the grill, butter already spread over it, sauce already made. She gave a funny little laugh, because in spite of her anxiety she felt hungry. Before she could decide whether to cook her fish or have another snack, there was a sharp ring at the front door bell, coming so unexpectedly that it startled her.

She turned to walk along the passage, but could make out no shape against the glass of the door.

Witzy wouldn't ring the bell.

She felt nervous, not in fear for herself, but in fear of what this might mean. She hesitated before opening the door, and the bell rang again. She did what Witzy had always told her to do: opened it on the chain, so that if the odd chance happened and this was a burglar, she would not be caught unprepared.

A tall man said: "I'm sorry to worry you. Is Detective Constable Birwitz in, please?"

She said: "No."

"I'm very anxious to see him," the man declared. "I'm from the *Daily Globe*. Do you know when he will be back?"

"He's gone to the pictures," Meg said, almost desperate.

"To the *pictures*?" The man sounded incredulous. "Tonight?"

"Why on earth shouldn't he go out tonight if he wants to?" she demanded hotly. And why should a man from one of the big national newspapers want to see Witz?

"I wouldn't have thought it anything to celebrate,"

the man said. "I'm perfectly harmless, Mrs Birwitz—
are you Mrs Birwitz?"

"Yes."

"May I come in and wait for him?"

There was no reason why not, except that Meg
didn't want anyone here; on the other hand, she was
anxious to ask questions, to find out what this man
could tell her. *What* wasn't anything to celebrate?

She slid the chain out of its channel, and opened the
door wider. The hall light shone on a man with fair
hair, which receded from his forehead showing that it
was conically shaped, a collar too large for him and a
tie with a big, clumsy knot. He gave her his card, and
she read:

Arthur A. Anvill
Daily Globe, Fleet Street.
Tel.: FLE 19061

Apparently he was what he claimed to be.

Meg stood aside, but before she stepped in, and while
he was looking at her curiously, footsteps sounded in
the street, and she recognised Witzy's.

"There he is!" she exclaimed.

The reporter turned on his heel. Witzy came hurrying, and there was something purposeful about his
stride. The light caught his eyes, and they seemed to
glitter. He gave a strange impression: that he was going
to walk straight into the newspaperman.

He stopped just in front of him, and demanded:

"What do you want?"

"Detective Birwitz? I'm from the *Globe*. I wonder if
you can spare me—?"

"Just get out," Witzy said. Meg could not remember
him speaking so harshly to anyone. "Stop bothering
me and my wife."

"Now in your own interests—" Anvill began.

"You can walk," Witz said, "or I can throw you
out." He sounded as if he would like to do that; there

was a harsh, quivering note in his voice, as if his whole body was shaking. He moved to one side, and for a moment Meg thought he was going to push the man but he did not.

Anvill moved a few feet, turning round so that he could see Witzy all the time, and tried again in a different tone.

"This isn't going to help you, Birwitz. The *Globe*'s taking the line that the police have to take too much lying down, that it's time a criminal caught in the act knows he'll get roughed up if he starts the rough stuff himself. We're on your side."

Witzy stood staring at the man for what seemed a long time. Meg moved out on to the porch, shivered under a blast of wind, but reached Witzy's side. She didn't touch him; she felt only that she wanted to be near him.

Witzy said: "I'm a police officer under suspension, and whether you're for or against me won't help when it comes to the Inquiry. If I talk to you or anyone else, they'll hold it against me."

Meg echoed to herself: *Suspension?* She was bewildered, and beginning to feel dismayed, but still didn't start to understand. How long had Witzy been under suspension? Was *this* what had been worrying him?

"Answer me one question," Anvill said. "Did you start the fight with this man Dibble, or did he start it?"

"He started it."

"How?"

"He tried to—" Witzy broke off, turned away, bumping into Meg, and went on stiffly: "One question, you said—I've answered it. Good-night." The last word was uttered under his breath. He went forward into the bungalow, watched by the newspaperman, who moved suddenly, gripped Meg's arm, and said in a low-pitched voice:

"He can't talk, but you can. Get the whole story out of him, and I'll see you tomorrow." He let her go, then turned and strode off.

Witzy was half-way towards the kitchen, moving very stiffly. Meg closed the door. Witzy hesitated in the kitchen doorway, as if he did not know what to do next.

She said: "Witz, what's happened?" and hurried towards him. He swung round, and blocked the doorway. For a moment she thought that he was going to strike her; the wild look was in his eyes again. She was appalled.

"Never mind asking questions," he said harshly. "Answer some. Answer one. Where were you at lunchtime? Who did you meet?" When she didn't answer at first, being so astonished, he moved forward, gripping the tops of her arms so tightly that it hurt. "Come on, let's have the truth. Who was he?"

5

REASON

ANGER rose up in Meg Birwitz as Witzy shouted the question; anger heightened by the pain, heightened by the way he raved, heightened by the fact that he bitterly distrusted her. And she had been on edge for him all the afternoon and evening, while what she had just learned had torn at her nerves.

In that moment, while he glared at her, demanding an answer, she felt that all she wanted to do was shout back, to hurt as he was hurting her. Then he began to shake her, not vigorously, but slowly, to and fro. His mouth was set tightly, his eyes held that unnatural brightness; as if he was sick. *Sick*. Then she understood at least one thing: that he wasn't himself, that something had happened which she did not know about, and that he was in need of help. If she raised her voice, it would lead to a quarrel which might go on and on;

only twice had they really quarrelled, and she hated the recollection.

He was still shaking her, slowly, steadily.

"Well, who was he? Just tell me who he was."

"Listen, darling," Meg said, and she did not know how she managed to keep her voice steady. "I had lunch with Dorothy Melson. If you look in my bag you'll find a Bentall's bill, with her telephone number on the back—I promised to call her. You call her, if you like."

Witzy's grip did not slacken, but he stopped shaking her. He seemed dumbstruck.

"If you'll tell me why you think I lied to you, it might help," Meg said.

Very slowly, he released her, and the glitter faded from his eyes. He turned round. She thought that he was going to her handbag, and for some reason she did not clearly understand, she would hate that; certainly it would prove how deep his suspicions went—suspicions of which she had never dreamed. She thought almost hysterically that this evening she had actually told herself there might be another woman. What was happening to them both?

Witzy went into the kitchen, and stretched out a hand, as if he couldn't see; he touched the edge of the table and came up against it and stood motionless. Meg went past him, and stood with her back to the working top where the soft white fish was ready and the sauce stood in its little silver-plated boat. She looked straight at her husband, seeing how he was clenching his teeth, thrusting his jaw forward, his eyes screwed up.

This wasn't the moment to speak, but she knew what to do. She went past him again, out of the kitchen, into the small dining-room. She opened the end of the sideboard, took out whisky and soda, and poured two drinks, one very strong, one fairly weak. She carried the two glasses into the kitchen. Witzy was standing in the same position, but was more relaxed.

"I think we need this," she said.

He opened his eyes and saw the glasses. His lips quivered. He muttered: "I know what I need," and took the glass she held out to him. He drank slowly, as if determined that he should not just gulp it down. Meg sipped. There was a sheen as of tears in his eyes, but his mouth was no longer taut and his eyes no longer screwed up.

He drank more whisky, put his glass down, and said: "Meg, we're in trouble, and I put us there. What would you like to know first?"

"Witzy—" she began, but found it difficult to go on. "Witzy, what's this about suspension?"

"I'm suspended, with full pay for the time being."

"But why?"

"The honest answer is that I—I bashed a man almost to pulp this afternoon." When Meg didn't respond, feeling too shocked, he went on: "A thief named Dibble, who'd already knocked out one of our chaps and tried to bring an oar down on my head. I saw red. I believe they had to pull me off him."

"Witzy," Meg said. That was all, and nothing else was needed. She wanted him to talk, to tell her everything. So far he was speaking in rather halting sentences, as if jeering at himself and wanting to hurt himself, but if she could encourage him to go on he would soon talk more freely, and that would help him.

"He's unconscious in hospital," Witzy went on. "They say he's on the danger list. A reporter saw what happened, and you know how sensitive the Old Man is to publicity. The long and short of it is that I was up on the carpet, and suspended. So the Old Man expects trouble. Dibble probably has a smart lawyer who'll see this as a chance to get some damages."

"But if he was a violent criminal—"

"He wasn't when I really started on him. I'd caught him and dragged him through the river. He was like a half-drowned rat, all the fight knocked out of him. But

it wasn't knocked out of me." The self-mockery was
very clear in Witzy's voice; a kind of self hatred. "I
think I wanted to kill him. I think he was a kind of
stand-in for the man I thought you'd had lunch with.
Meg—give me a straight answer. I can take it. I
promise not to choke the life out of you, or anything
like that. Is there another man?"

She thought: It's going to be all right now. She knew
that whatever came they could work it out together.
All she had to do was convince him, once and for all,
how wrong his suspicions were.

She said very steadily: "No, darling. There never has
been. There couldn't be. I love you too much."

His lips were working.

He muttered: "Oh, God!" and moved towards her
as she moved to him. She had never known the grip
of his arms so powerful, never known him struggle for
breath as he did now; in fact he was trying to make sure
that he didn't break down. If he broke down he would
probably feel some sense of weakness, even of shame.
She could hear his teeth grinding with the physical
effort, until at last she sensed that the tension was
beginning to flow out of him.

*   *   *   *   *

He was sitting one side of the kitchen table, Meg
the other. They had finished eating an hour or more
ago. Their coffee cups were empty. The only sound
except of their voices was in the whining wind outside.

Birwitz had talked almost without ceasing since that
moment of understanding; at first too quickly, soon
much more rationally. The morning's anonymous
letter lay on the table between them. Birwitz thought
he would always remember Meg's expression when she
read it, and he would always condemn himself for
giving it a second thought. In a way, he felt worse
because she hadn't uttered a word of reproach.

He realised that it would have been more difficult

without the second problem, which was the main one:
his suspension. No one else but Meg understood the
intensity of his devotion to the Force; no one could
understand that his job was really a vocation. Loving
her, working against the criminals—it didn't matter
what he did; he was always a hundred per center. Now,
although talking eased the situation, he was beginning
to feel the chill danger for their future.

". . . it just got into me. I know I was a bloody fool,
but how can I explain that to the Old Man, or to this
Inquiry? The devil of it is that I'm caught either way.
They'll say that if I can allow my private affairs to
affect my job so much, I can't have what it takes to be
a good policeman. Q.E.D. And if I let fly like I did at
Dibble, ditto." Birwitz pushed his chair back and
stood up. "Now you see the full extent of it, Meg. Now
you see what an absolute and utter lunatic I've been.
What the hell am I to do?"

Meg was still sitting there, flaxen hair brushed back
from her face, cheek-bones a little prominent, eyes a
little sunken; a statue of a woman carved by a Scandinavian master. Her hands were clasped on the table
in front of her, within a few inches of the typewritten
letter.

"There's one certain thing, darling," she said.
"You've got to show them that you were justified in
attacking the man."

"Meg."

"Yes?"

"I wasn't."

"I know you weren't, in the end," Meg said, quietly.
"But you had some justification in the beginning. The
newspapers are going to make this out to be much worse
than it is, aren't they? They're going to exaggerate it."

"I can't say I blame them."

"Then if they exaggerate what you actually did, you
must exaggerate your side of it," Meg argued. Birwitz
could tell that she was afraid he wouldn't agree; in a

way she was pleading for him to listen to her argument.
"There's nothing wrong in that. You didn't have any
reason to attack the man like you did, but you can say
at the time you *thought* you had. And there was Manny
—darling, listen! Only the night before your closest
friend had been shot. No wonder you were on edge.
What would have happened if this man had taken out a
gun? Would you have been blamed for what you did?"

Birwitz thought: And I didn't realise my good luck.
He gave a high-pitched laugh, his first since he had
come home, moved across to her, and tipped her head
back, his right hand beneath her chin. He looked into
her eyes.

"No," he said. "If he'd shown a gun, it wouldn't
have mattered if I'd killed him. But he didn't."

"You could have thought he was going to get one
out of his pocket!"

"Meg, Meg," Birwitz said, thickly. He lowered his
face until their lips touched. He kissed her gently at
first, then harder and with passion; and his hand moved
from her chin to her breast. He held her like that, so
that they could breath only through their nostrils, and
soon he felt the hardness of her teeth on his lips. He
drew back a fraction of an inch.

"Let's go upstairs," he whispered hoarsely. "Show
me you've really forgiven me. Come on!" he kissed
her again and then drew back, placed his hands beneath
her elbows, and began to raise her to her feet. "Meg—"

"No!" Meg said. "No, not now—*Witz, listen to me!*
I must telephone that man Anvill and tell him you've
told me that you thought Dibble was going to draw
a gun. You can't tell him that, you'd have to tell
Nunn, but *I* can tell the newspaper. If that's in the
Globe tomorrow morning it's bound to help. No one
can prove that it's not the truth, not the whole truth."

Birwitz stood back from her; shamed.

"You're right," he said. "Time for passion comes
later!" Meg was standing up now, and began to move

towards the telephone which was in the passage, handy for all the rooms. "Where's that card he gave you?" Birwitz demanded. "I'll dial the number." He gave the high-pitched laugh again. "This is what you call fighting for your life!"

Meg held out the card. Birwitz dialled, then handed the instrument to her. He stood by her side, arms round her, hugging her, as she asked for Anvill. She held on for a long time, and it seemed as if the man must be out. Soon he heard a voice come faintly from the ear-piece, and saw Meg tense.

"Mr. Anvill?" There was a pause; then she darted a glance and a smile at Birwitz. "Mr. Anvill, this is Mrs. Birwitz. I've had a long talk with my husband, and there's something he wouldn't tell his superior, because it sounds so like an excuse, but which I think you ought to know. . . . Yes, I'm sure it is important. . . . Yes, I'll wait a moment." She pressed the earpiece against her breast. "It'll be all right, darling!"

She talked for ten minutes, answering searching questions, sometimes referring to Birwitz for the answers. When she rang off, she stood looking at her husband, her eyes very wide open. In a curious way this seemed to have affected her more than anything else; she leaned against the wall as if she were exhausted.

"Come on, sweet," Birwitz said. "Let's go to bed. You're tired out. I'll bring you a cup of warm milk . . ."

*　　*　　*　　*　　*

"Witz," she said, as she sat up on the pillows, and the steam from the milk wafted like smoke about her mouth and nose, "there's still the most important thing."

"Most important?"

"In a way."

"I don't get it," Birwitz said.

She sipped the milk, and between sips said slowly: "No, I don't believe you do, darling. You've almost forgotten it. That letter."

Birwitz said: "I tell you that if I get a letter a day for a month I'll simply tear it up and throw it away!"

"Yes, you probably would, but—"

Birwitz exclaimed suddenly: "Good God! Yes."

"You see what I mean?"

"I see exactly what you mean. I also see what a bad policeman I make."

"It's no use talking like that."

"If I face up to the truth it might help later," Birwitz said bitterly. "Who wrote the letters?"

"Yes."

"And why?"

"Witz," Meg asked, "who hates us? Who wants to try to break up our marriage?"

"It doesn't make any sense."

"How many letters have you had?"

"Ten."

"Who's sending them, Witz?"

"I'm going to find out."

"Witz."

"Yes?"

"You ought to tell Nunn."

"You know what I'd like to do to Nunn."

"I know," said Meg. "But you've already admitted that he didn't really have any choice about suspending you. Witz, you ought to tell him. Ask him to come and see you in the morning, or to see you at the station. We've got to find out who sent them, and what he's trying to do."

6

JOB FOR WEST

ROGER WEST stepped into his office on the morning after his visit to Nunn's division, and went across to the window which overlooked the Thames. The Chief

Inspector who served as his chief assistant, a man
named Cope, wasn't in; he had been out very late the
night before.

Outside, a wind of exceptional force was whipping
the Thames to sea-sized waves. Men and women were
holding on to their hats and bending against the storm.
A young girl wearing a plastic raincoat had it moulded
so close to her body that it looked as if she were a
silver sculpture. Roger had never seen the Thames so
rough, nor the sky so glowering; yet it wasn't raining.

He glanced through the reports on his desk, but
there was nothing new of importance, except the report
from Richmond on Birwitz.

One of the two telephones on his desk rang.

"West speaking."

"Come and see me, Handsome, will you?" It was
the Assistant Commissioner, Hardy. The use of the
'Handsome' indicated his mood; it was as likely to be
West if he were worried or annoyed about anything.

"Can I have ten minutes?" Roger asked.

"Don't make it longer."

"Right, sir," Roger said. The occasional 'sir' was a
good thing with Hardy, who had come up from the
ranks and was resented by some of the older men
because of it. Hardy was a man without close friends
or *confidants* at the Yard. Roger was probably the
nearest he had to either; but there was something about
Hardy which made it difficult to get to know him.

Roger thumbed through the Birwitz report again,
then put in a call to the Richmond Hospital, to inquire
about Dibble.

"He's out of danger, Mr. West," the hospital secretary said.

"Is that certain?"

"There's no danger at all now—the wounds weren't
as bad as we first thought."

"Good," said Roger. "Many thanks." He put in a
call to Nunn, but was told that Nunn was out and

would ring him back. He sent for a sergeant to take over while the office was empty, took the Birwitz report, and went along to Hardy's office.

This was on the floor below, much bigger and more attractive than Roger's, overlooking the Embankment but without such a good view. The heavy boughs of plane trees just outside the window were bent almost double.

Hardy, a broad-shouldered, fairly thick-set man with grey hair, wore a good fitting grey suit, and had a scrubbed look; he was always immaculate, as if that was a way of justifying his position.

"Ah," he said. "Come and sit down." He had several newspapers spread out on a table by the side of his desk; four of the five headlined the Birwitz 'attack' on the man Dibble, who was said to be at death's door. "How's this man Dibble?"

"He'll come through."

"That's a relief," said Hardy. "If he died we would have a rough time with the Press, and we don't want it just now. Didn't you say you saw Birwitz yesterday?"

"Yes."

"What did you make of him?"

"Taut as a stretched wire."

"Any idea why?"

"No," replied Roger. "But I'm going to find out, today with any luck. Nunn gave me his blessing. I would have gone to see Birwitz last night, but I decided it was bad timing. Of course it could be simple coincidence."

"Probably is," conceded Hardy. He picked up a thick red pencil and pointed to the newspapers. "Seen these?"

"Every one."

"The *Globe*'s on our side, anyhow."

"It's a pity Dibble didn't have a gun in his pocket," Roger said. He leaned back in his chair. "The *Globe*'s careful to quote only Birwitz's wife. It looks as if

Birwitz kept his head after he left Nunn's office—he was pretty mad then. I'll see him today."

Hardy rolled his pencil between thumb and fore-finger and it flashed as bright as neon. He pursed his lips, making them very full. A lot of the Yard men thought that habit was a pose; Roger believed it showed that Hardy was really puzzled, and trying to work the situation out.

"Do that," he said at last. "But don't let's white-wash him, Handsome. If he thought this chap was going to pull a gun, that's one thing. If he didn't, that's another. I can see this becoming a Home Office Inquiry if we don't handle it right. At best there'll be a lot of questions in the House, with trouble storing up for us if we put Birwitz back on duty and another of our chaps loses his head. I'm inclined to think that it might be a good idea to go all the way with Birwitz—make it obvious that we aren't going to tolerate the use of unnecessary violence. So make sure whether he's lying, won't you?"

Roger said: "I'll make sure." He didn't get up, but sat and studied Hardy, feeling sure that the A.C. hadn't yet finished. "And I'll report by tomorrow."

"Good," said Hardy. "Then there's this other trouble. I don't like it—don't like it a bit. If this reached the ears of the Press, coming on top of the Birwitz affair, it would really set the cat among the pigeons."

It was like Hardy to talk obliquely; like West to come right out into the open when he made sure that Hardy wasn't going to say anything more.

"We now have five men suspected of taking bribes, and soft pedalling on their evidence," he said flatly, "and if we've five under suspicion, fifty might be involved."

Hardy was rolling the pencil very quickly.

"It's a nasty situation," he said. "The Commis-sioner's asked me for a full report by the end of next week. He wants me to detail one man to do the job, Handsome. You're the man."

"You're the boss."

"Glad you take it that way," Hardy said, thus explaining why he had been ill at ease. "Not a very pleasant job, I know. Snooping on our own chaps. You're not going to like it, but if there is any large-scale corruption we've got to find out. How far will you go with the Divisional Supers?"

"I'll tell them a little, let them think it's an isolated case now and again," Roger said. "Er—" he broke off, half smiling.

"Yes?"

"May I have a free hand?"

Hardy stared; then gave an unexpected and broad smile.

"You mean, will I leave it to you to decide what you tell the others? Yes, all right, Handsome. It's in your hands. I'm only anxious that you shouldn't be known as the man who's on this job. Once it's known, you'll be fed with a lot of phoney stuff to put you off the scent."

"Yes," agreed Roger, and asked straightly: "You think corruption's pretty rife, don't you?"

"Wouldn't go that far. Just afraid that it might be," said Hardy. "After all, the fact is, we've lost five straightforward cases, each in a different division, because the police witness changed his story in the box. Under pressure, I know. This Birwitz. Would you say he'd changed his story?"

"He didn't put it over well, anyhow."

"Well, all right," said Hardy, standing up. Quite unexpectedly, he held out his hand. "Thanks, Handsome. It's the kind of job I used to get landed with, years ago. In fact I had one rather like it, fairly early in my inspectorship days. Half the reason why some of the chaps would like to see me retired is because of that. Had to make myself damned unpleasant sometimes, and—you remember Kennedy, don't you?"

"Yes," said Roger quietly. "I shouldn't lose any

sleep over him. He made out all right after he left the
Force. He should never have been a copper."

"He was a friend of mine," Hardy said awkwardly.
"After he was fired, it wasn't easy to make other
friends. Never has been for me. But what could I do?
If I'd tipped him off, and he'd stopped playing the
fool for a while, he would probably have started
again." Hardy stared straight ahead of him as if he
were thinking back to those hard, harsh days. Then he
braced himself. "You'll probably find a better way of
going about it." He went with Roger to the door. "Let
me know from time to time. No need to report every
day. Oh—shift your other jobs on to someone else."

"I'd much rather not," Roger said.

"Why not?"

"If I do, everyone'll know I've a special assignment.
And if I've got one that I won't talk about, a lot of
people will begin to put two and two together."

"Handle it your own way," conceded Hardy rue-
fully. "You will, anyway." He nodded, and opened
the door.

Roger went out into the passage, where three other
superintendents were standing and talking. As he went
up, one of them, an old friend named Sloan, raised a
hand in greeting and said:

"We're just deciding whether Birwitz ought to be
hung, drawn, or quartered."

"Read the *Globe*?" inquired Roger.

"You don't believe that whitewash, do you?"

"I'm going to find out," said Roger. "Hardy's told
me to go and see Birwitz again." He went along to his
own office with a chorus of laughter following him; a
light-hearted laughter, but with a note almost of
mockery in it.

Very few men at the Yard doubted that Birwitz
had lost his self-control, and that every one of them
would feel some of the repercussions. Birwitz wasn't
likely to be popular anywhere in the Force.

In Roger's office, the sergeant was still on duty; Dave Cope hadn't arrived. Roger put in a call to the *Daily Globe*, and while he was waiting for it to come in, checked the case against Dibble. There was a note from the Legal Department asking for a detailed account for the Public Prosecutor's office, and did he think the charge should be one of attempted murder?

Roger wrote: "Yes, emphatically," across this, and pinned it to the reports.

Then the *Globe* came through, and he asked for Anvill, half expecting to learn that the reporter hadn't yet come in. But Anvill answered.

"Who's that?"

"West of the Yard," Roger said. "Remember me?"

"Yes, Mr. West," said Anvill. He was an old acquaintance rather than an old friend. He had a reputation for being ruthless but completely fair; Roger knew that unless he felt sure his information was right, he never used it. "Don't tell me you want some help from a newspaperman."

"Just an opinion," Roger said, mildly.

"Birwitz?"

"Yes."

"In the first place, I ought to tell you that the *Globe* is rooting for Birwitz. We're claiming he ought to be taken off the suspension list right away, since otherwise it's an encouragement to all violent-minded slobs to take a crack at a copper whenever they like."

"Thanks," said Roger.

"And you want to know what I think of Birwitz personally?"

"I do," agreed Roger. It was wise to play this straight. If he answered lightly, he might put this man in the wrong mood. "You're as good as a customs officer in sizing men up."

Anvill didn't answer at once.

"Aren't you?" Roger asked, and wondered if he was overdoing the butter.

"Birwitz had a chip on his shoulder last night," said Anvill, slowly but positively. "I thought he was going to give me the treatment, too. He probably would have done if his wife hadn't been around. She's really something, in a bold Scandinavian way. She told me she wormed the story about Dibble going for a gun out of hubby. He was so full of stinking pride and anger with the Metropolitan Police Force that nothing would have made him talk about it if she hadn't worked on him. That could easily be true. She swears it is, anyhow. Birwitz hasn't confirmed one way or the other." Anvill paused. "That help at all?"

"Thanks," Roger said.

"You in charge of the case?"

"I'm investigating a series of crimes like Hobber's, trying to find out if they're organised, and that will take me over to Richmond a lot, so I'm fitting Birwitz in," said Roger. "How about your friends in Fleet Street?"

"The other papers, do you mean?"

"Yes."

"Solid against Birwitz. He gave a lot of them the brush-off yesterday. When are coppers going to learn that the gentlemen of the Press have their feelings?"

Roger laughed.

"As soon as they realise that all policemen are human beings at heart!" He rang off before Anvill could make a come-back and was smiling when the door opened and Cope came in.

Cope was a thin, spindly Cockney, with a brisk and breezy manner, a lively sense of humour and a remarkable aptitude for remembering detail. He was the ideal second-in-command, and the time would come when he would have to be told about the main job Roger was now working on; but the time was not yet.

"I think everything's shipshape," Roger said. "I'm going over to see Nunn. Let him know I'm on the way, will you?"

"Oke," said Cope. "Kick Birwitz in the pants for

me." He dropped into his chair, and began to loosen his red and white spotted tie. "Have you heard what happened over at Marlborough Street this morning?"

Roger said sharply: "No. What?"

"We had Widderman on toast," said Cope; obviously he was annoyed in spite of his flippancy. "We've been trying to get him for organised vice for months, you know that, and he was up last night for gaming. He elected to be dealt with summarily. I thought he was bound to get a couple of months."

"Didn't he?"

"Discharged."

"Why?" asked Roger. He felt very tense; he was almost sure what the answer would be.

"The younger of the two men we put up boobed in his evidence," Cope said. "Widderman's solicitor claimed that he came in after the raid. One of our chaps swore he'd been there when they arrived. The other let himself be caught out by a smart young lawman, so there was some doubt. The others all got fined. Widderman said his flat was used for the gambling without his knowledge, and got off. Evidence is evidence and doubt is doubt. You know what, Handsome?"

Roger said: "I know I'd like to find out the name of that smart young lawman. It couldn't be the one involved in any of the other cases that have gone against us, could it?"

"I'll find out," promised Cope. "Know what I think?"

"Tell me."

"I think there's a move on foot to discredit police witnesses, and it wouldn't surprise me if it's pretty widespread. That's what makes me so mad at Birwitz. The quicker he's chucked out of the Force so that the Great British Public knows we won't stand any nonsense, the better."

"You may be right," said Roger, and went out.

7

TIGHTROPE

ONE thing was immediately obvious to Roger; he was
going to have to walk a tightrope. A lot of senior men
were the over-sensitive ones at the Yard and in the
Divisions, and they would resent any implication that
they or any of their staff might be taking bribes. There
were others who would soon put two and two together,
and begin to ask why the Commissioner wasn't 'taking
steps'. Some bright newspaperman, possibly Anvill,
would start to work on the same angle.

At the moment there were the five original cases,
Birwitz making the sixth, and the Widderman case the
seventh; each might be quite isolated, but there was a
reasonable chance of some thread running through
them all.

Roger tucked himself into the driving seat of his car,
slammed the door, and edged out of the Yard. A plain-
clothes man and a uniformed sergeant were at the gates;
the sergeant saw that the road was clear. It was almost
possible to hear what the sergeant was thinking: There's
West going off without a driver again. There were
advantages and disadvantages in having that kind of
lone wolf reputation.

Roger headed for Fulham, along the Embankment,
finding it difficult to think about the job in hand. Now
and again, water smacked against the river defences and
shot towers of spray on to the pavement and into the
road. Pools of river water were gathering in the gutters.
In patches the traffic had to move very slowly. Here and
there small groups of policemen, firemen and Civil
Defence workers stood about, where the water was
deepest. There was real anxiety about breaches in the

Embankment, because the river had been high before
this gale.

A man crossing the road was caught in a sudden gust
of wind, and sent staggering in front of a cyclist; they
collided. The man fell, and his hat was whipped from
his head, showing him to be old and almost bald. Three
people turned to help him. Now and again Roger felt a
gust of wind side swipe the car so hard that it turned
the wheel in his hands.

He was glad to get away from the river and into the
comparative shelter of roads with houses on either side.
Paper, hats, umbrellas, cardboard boxes, the winter's
dark leaves, were dancing about in miniature whirl-
winds.

Roger passed the end of Bell Street, where he lived,
and conquered the temptation to call in for a cup of
coffee. He was crossing Putney Bridge, where people
lined the parapet, staring at the rampaging river below,
when his radio crackled and his name was called.

He flicked into communication.

"West speaking, over to you."

"Information for you, Mr. West. . . . This is Information, reporting that Superintendent Nunn would like
to see you as soon as possible."

"Tell him I'm on my way to see him."

"Very good, sir. That is all."

Roger flicked off, wondered why Cope hadn't given
him that message, wondered what Nunn wanted, then
he began to concentrate on the seven cases—mostly on
the first five, since the other two were still in progress.

Two Yard officers, of junior rank, had slipped up
badly in giving evidence. So had one man from the
Whitechapel Division, one from Lambeth, one from
Hampstead—and now the men in Richmond and the
Central Division. In each case the pattern was the
same—an officer believed to be a completely sound and
reliable witness had allowed himself to be caught out in
a lie, or at least in indecision, thus destroying the value

of his evidence. It was such an easy way of picking up a hundred pounds; but there wasn't yet any proof at all.

Roger considered the cases themselves, and the accused. Leaving out Mrs. Haughton and Widderman, the one believed to be a respectable middle-class matron and the other suspected of being an organiser of gambling, prostitution and vice in general, what had the accused had in common?

The Whitechapel man had been a pawnbroker accused of receiving stolen goods.

The Lambeth man had been a bookmaker accused of having a ring of street runners.

The Hampstead case had been against a woman accused of fraud under hire purchase agreements— signing agreements, obtaining possession of television sets, vacuum cleaners and other household goods, and selling them for cash.

The two Yard cases had been dissimilar, too. One, a man accused of company frauds; a very intricate case indeed which, by itself, would not have seemed remarkable. The other, a simple charge of robbery with violence, and the evidence had turned on identification.

It was difficult to think of a greater assortment of cases, almost ridiculous to consider that they might be connected.

Roger had studied the records, the build-up of the cases, and verbatim reports of the hearings and the evidence which had fallen down, but he had not yet interviewed any of the men concerned. There was one common denominator; in each case the defending solicitor had been described as 'young'—but all the names were different.

Roger turned into Richmond High Street as his radio crackled again.

"West speaking."

"Aye aye, sir." Only Cope would talk like that. "Got the names of the two young pups you're after—those solicitors."

"Yes?"

"Cartwright at Richmond, Samson at Marlborough Street."

"All right," Roger said. "Check to find out if there is any kind of association between the two firms they work for, will you?"

"Aye, aye, sir."

Roger could not recall men named Cartwright or Samson in any of the cases he had heard himself.

He turned towards the residential riverside part of the district, deliberately going the long way round, so as to make sure there was nothing he had forgotten so far as Nunn and the Birwitz business was concerned. Then he drove round to the police station. Obviously he was expected. Men saluted, and he made a point of acknowledging each one.

Upstairs, a nice-looking girl secretary said:

"Mr. Nunn's expecting you, Mr. West. Will you go straight in?"

"Yes, thanks."

Roger sensed a mood of excitement which he did not think was imaginary, and was soon sure that Nunn had something on his mind. He stood up, hand outstretched; as Roger sat down the secretary brought in tea in a brown ware pot, and some biscuits.

"Waited tea for you," said Nunn. He was getting too fat. There was a criss-cross of purply veins on his cheeks which suggested too much spirit drinking, or else high blood pressure; but his voice was controlled enough. He poured out. "Something very peculiar's turned up about young Birwitz," he announced. "I don't quite know what to make of it, and I thought you ought to know pretty quickly."

"Thanks."

"He came round to see me this morning," Nunn said. "Seemed a different chap from yesterday afternoon, when I thought he was going to dot me one. He'd slept on things and seen what a fool he'd made of himself, but when he told me his story I could at least understand what got into him." Nunn pushed a crumpled looking typewritten letter across his desk; it was a poor quality notepaper. "He'd received that yesterday morning. It was his tenth. He admits that he half-believed there was something in it, and—" Nunn shrugged, as if to let Roger judge for himself.

Roger read the letter, and asked: "Anything in the accusation?"

"This morning Birwitz says he can't understand what made him think it was even possible. He had a long talk with his wife and she's convinced him that it's all baloney."

"Do you think it is?"

"Couldn't be sure, that's why I didn't call you at once," replied Nunn. "I checked with the fellows who know Birwitz well—even went to the hospital to see our uniformed chap who was shot—Manny Thompson was Birwitz's oldest friend. Every report is the same. Matilda, known as Meg, Birwitz is a one-man woman. They've been married nearly four years. They've paid for their house—bungalow rather—and everything in it. According to Thompson, they've just started thinking about a family. Very house-proud woman—half-Swedish, half-English, but lived in England all her life. No one thinks there's any possibility of this boy-friend being true. I've got a couple of chaps checking among tradespeople, and—" Nunn broke off again.

"You think she'll turn up with a clean record?" said Roger, thoughtfully.

"Yes."

"Yet Birwitz—"

"You can't expect me to answer for Birwitz," Nunn protested. "I don't even know what goes on in his mind. And if you worship a woman as he seems to worship his wife, and you get a few of these pieces of filth, well—it speaks for itself."

Roger said: "When did he get this one?"

"Yesterday morning."

"Coincidence, I wonder? Have you got the background of that Haughton woman?"

"Yes—all here," said Nunn, slapping his hand on a manilla folder. There were not many papers in it.

"What do you know about the solicitor, young Cartwright?"

"He's pretty new," said Nunn, frowning in concentration. "I'd never come across him before, but my chaps tell me he's taken a few cases, all for the defence. He states his case well, and doesn't overdo the spouting, knowing that local benches don't like it. In his late twenties, apparently, and a junior partner in a Wimbledon firm."

"Do you know if his firm represents Mrs. Haughton in normal business?"

"No, but I'll find out."

"Thanks," said Roger. "Can we do anything more against Mrs. H.? Find any other charge, for instance, or anything we might reasonably talk to her about?"

"I don't want to touch her with a barge-pole. She's already talking about wrongful arrest, and if we get under her skin she might have a go at us. Last thing we want." What Nunn meant was that he did not want that kind of trouble in his last few months in the Force. That was easy to understand. "What have you got in mind?"

"Nothing, yet," temporised Roger. "Where's Birwitz?"

"I sent him home. He can be here in twenty minutes if you want him."

"I think I'd rather go and see him, and size up his wife, too," said Roger. He picked up the typewritten letter, scanned it again, and went on: "Mrs. H. got a typewriter?"

Nunn exclaimed: "Good God!"

"Has she?"

"It hasn't occurred to me to find out, but—" Nunn broke off. "I certainly will, though."

"And can you get some photostat copies of the letter,

so that we can check typewriters against it?" asked
Roger. He made no other comment, but he saw in this
development a possibility which might carry him a long
way across that tightrope. "If I could pick up a dozen
later, I'd be grateful."

"I'll fix it," promised Nunn. "How about lunch,
Handsome? There's a nice little pub on the river".

"Can I leave saying 'yes' until after I've seen Birwitz?"

"I'll book a table, in case you're able to come," Nunn
said. He looked up as something rapped sharply against
the window; a twig, or leaf, hard driven by the wind.
"Hell of a morning, isn't it?"

"Yes," said Roger, absently.

He felt a gust catch at the tail of his coat as he went
out, after studying a map of the district and making sure
that he knew the way to the Birwitzs' house in Hillrock
Avenue. The supple young trees lining the street were
bent almost double. All the picturesque attractiveness
one would find here on a sunny day was despoiled.

A man turned the corner, on foot, just behind him;
he noticed that without thinking anything of it.

The small garden in front of the Birwitz bungalow
looked as neat as a garden could do in face of the wind's
destructive wildness. The bungalow looked freshly
painted, a little place to be proud of.

Roger rang the bell, heard a man's footsteps almost
at once, and then heard Birwitz call out: "*Shut the back
door, Meg!*" A moment later this door opened, and
Birwitz faced Roger. Obviously he recognised him on
the instant. He froze.

"Good—good-morning, sir."

" 'Morning, Birwitz," Roger said briskly. "I'd like a
word with you."

"Who is it?" called a woman, from the other end of
the bungalow.

Birwitz began: "It's Chief Superintendent—" and
broke off. "Come in, please." He stood aside as wind
rattled two small, black-framed pictures on the passage

wall, and led the way into the front room. Here was modern furniture of Scandinavian type, bright, plain colours against a pale grey carpet—with what Janet would call 'a touch about it'. The woman's footsteps tapped on the floor, and Birwitz, getting over his surprise, turned to face his wife: "Meg, it's Mr. West of Scotland Yard. Leave us alone for a bit, will you?"

The woman appeared in the doorway, and Roger saw at once what Nunn meant about her. In her rather big-boned, almost gaunt way she was extremely attractive; a Katherine Hepburn of a woman.

"Good-morning, Mr. West," she said; he was vaguely surprised that her voice held no trace of accent. She stood hesitating. Then: "Would you like some coffee?"

Roger said: "No, thanks, Mrs. Birwitz, but I'd like you to be present. I'm here partly about the poison pen letters, partly about what happened yesterday." He noticed the way the couple glanced at each other, with that kind of affinity of reaction which sometimes exists between husband and wife but is not necessarily conspiratorial. "I'm on my own. You know as well as I do, Birwitz, that nothing you say to me while I'm here alone can be formally reported or held against you. I would like some blunt answers to some blunt questions, from both of you. Have you any objection to this kind of interrogation?"

It was the woman who said: "We'll welcome it. Won't we, Witz?"

8

INTERROGATION

"RIGHT," said Roger, very briskly. "Mrs. Birwitz, if you've anything to do in the kitchen, I can wait five minutes."

"I ought to turn the oven down," the woman said. "If you hadn't said that I'd have forgotten. I won't be a minute." She turned and hurried out, lithe-moving, her legs shapely but a little too big at the calves.

Birwitz seemed more affected by Roger's presence than his wife had been, but suddenly woke up, turned round and picked a yellow pine box off a small table, and opened it. "Cigarette, sir?"

"Thanks," said Roger. "In a minute, may I? Nip out the back way and see if anyone's about."

"Eh?"

"I think there was a man at the end of the street when I came round the corner, and I had a feeling that he began to move after I'd come in your gate. Don't give anything away, will you?"

"I won't," promised Birwitz. Although startled, he moved very quickly; already he had created a good impression. Roger heard him speak to his wife, then a door slammed in the wind.

Roger helped himself to a cigarette, and stood so that he could see a reflection of the street in the mirror which hung low and wide over the stone fireplace, a miniature inglenook. He saw a pedal cyclist battling against the wind, and then saw a short, thin man, bare-headed. Head down as the wind blew into his face, raincoat pressed against his body, he carried a long, narrow case.

Birwitz appeared, taking long strides, looking almost ungainly, nothing like so graceful as his wife. He went straight to the front gate, which was banging. The bare-headed man passed him, glancing up but making no comment. Birwitz pretended to have a lot of trouble fastening the gate, but turned back at last. A minute or two later, he came into the room, hair brushed back with his fingers, eyes watering from the wind. His wife was just behind him.

"That's queer," he remarked.

"What is?" asked Meg Birwitz.

"That chap in the street," Birwitz said. "I saw him here yesterday."

"Sure?" asked Roger.

"Yes. Selling brushes."

"You mean that man with the black arm-band?" demanded Meg.

"Yes," said Birwitz, and looked straight at Roger. "I didn't notice very much yesterday, sir, but I did see this chap—he was at a house a few doors along, and I saw him showing his brushes. What time did he call here, Meg?"

"Half past eleven," answered Meg. "He might have had an order, and come back to deliver it today, though."

Roger asked: "May I use your telephone?"

They were both anxious to show him where it was. He dialled the local headquarters and asked for Nunn, who came on the line at once. Roger described the brush salesman and his case, and went on: "I shouldn't pick him up, just have him tailed. Will you?"

Nunn said: "I'll fix it."

"Thanks." Roger rang off, and turned to face the Birwitzs.

He was taller than the local man, and nearly as fair as Meg, although grey was taking some of the sheen from his hair. He was good-looking in an almost too Hollywood way. The name 'Handsome' had been given him flippantly in his early days in the Force, and had stuck. There was about him an alertness, a briskness, a directness, which explained the fact that for years he had been the youngest Chief Inspector; for years he had been the youngest Chief Superintendent in the C.I.D., too. He was probably the best known man at the Yard. His sobriquet, and the fact that he was given so many off-beat jobs, gained him twice as much publicity as anyone else.

Birwitz knew most of this; and knew that in spite of

it all, Roger was popular with the Yard and at the Divisions.

*   *   *   *   *

Meg thought: If anyone can help us, surely he can.

*   *   *   *   *

"Now," said Roger, briskly, "let's try to get at some facts. Birwitz—how long have you known the woman Haughton?"

"Forty-eight hours," answered Birwitz.

"So you first saw her at Witt's Store?"

"Yes."

"Positive?"

"Yes."

"Not lying, are you?" Roger asked roughly and saw Birwitz's eyes narrow, resentment showing for the first time.

"No."

"Let's have it again. Had you ever seen the woman Haughton before you were called to the store?"

"No," said Birwitz, stiffly.

"Ever seen her in the street, or anywhere else?"

"No."

"It's a funny thing," Meg interpolated, as if anxious to ease the tension. "But I've often seen her when I've been out shopping. I recognised her photograph in the local newspaper this morning."

"Well, I haven't seen her," Birwitz insisted.

"Witz—"

"If your husband is going to get chipped every time he's asked a question he doesn't like, he isn't going to help himself or us," Roger said. He let that hang fire for a few moments, then went on: "Birwitz, had you seen the solicitor Cartwright before?"

"Yes."

"Where?"

"In court, defending two motoring cases."

"Did he get the verdicts?"

"He got one."

"Have you ever seen him out of court?"

"I saw him getting out of his car outside the court yesterday."

"Anywhere else?"

"No."

"How much did he pay you to fiddle your evidence against Mrs. Haughton?"

Meg exclaimed: "*No!*" and suddenly anger blazed in her eyes. Curiously, the question seemed to take Birwitz by surprise; perhaps Roger's sharp reproof had made him take a firmer grip on himself. He did not raise his voice, or stiffen, but answered quite mildly:

"I've never taken any bribe of any kind."

"Have you ever been offered bribes?"

"Yes."

"By whom?"

"A street bookmaker, and a buyer of stolen goods—both when I arrested them."

"When was this?"

"Last year."

"Were you offered any bribe over the Haughton case?"

"No."

"Did you see the woman take those goods?"

"I told the court—"

"Just answer me."

"I saw her."

"Why did you make a mess of giving your evidence?"

"Now, really, I can't stand—" Meg began.

"Please be quiet, Mrs. Birwitz."

"All right, Meg," Birwitz said, and answered evenly. "I was pretty worked up, Mr. West."

"What about?"

"Really—"

"Meg, please! About the poison pen letter."

"When did you get it?"

"By the morning post."

"Did you speak to your wife about it?"

"No."

"Why not?"

"Because—because I couldn't bring myself to."

"Did you mention the other letters to her?"

"No—not until last night."

"Is that how much you trusted her?"

"Mr. West, I won't have you—"

"*Please be quiet, Mrs. Birwitz.* Birwitz, did you trust your wife so little that you couldn't bring yourself to show her these foul letters which accused her of being a whore and a slut?"

"*Don't talk about my wife like that!*"

Roger stared at Birwitz coldly, as coldly at his wife, and then went on in a frigid voice:

"Let me put it another way. You had such trust in your wife's faithfulness and love for you that you withheld all information about these letters, and were so upset by this one that you made a complete hash of a straightforward task of giving evidence in a cut-and-dried case. Is that true or isn't it?"

Birwitz's eyes were glittering.

"If that's the way you want to put it."

"That's how it was. You didn't trust your wife."

"*What do you think you're trying to do?*" cried Meg. Her fists were clenched, her eyes brighter and more glittering even than her husband's.

Roger swung round on her.

"Did he trust you?"

"What are you trying—?"

"*Did he trust you?*"

"He—"

Birwitz said: "So I didn't trust my wife enough to burn those letters or forget about them. Would you—?"

Roger was staring at the woman as he rapped out the next question:

"Who bribed you to work on your husband's nerves so much that—"

"Don't talk to me like that!"

"Who bribed you?"

"No one bribed me! I wouldn't touch a penny of anyone's filthy money!"

For a moment it looked as if Meg could strike Roger; as if Birwitz would gladly join in. They stood in a triangle, Roger with his back to the window, but seeing the mirror, the woman on his right, Birwitz on his left—tall, angry, seething.

Then:

"No," Roger said in a completely different tone, "I don't believe you would, Mrs. Birwitz. Birwitz, let's try to get this absolutely straight. You want me to believe that the reason you dithered in the witness box yesterday, the reason you let that case slide out of our fingers, was preoccupation with this letter—in other words, unreasoning jealousy sparked by the fear that the letter might have some basis of truth. Is that the only reason?"

"Yes," Birwitz said huskily.

"And did you realise that the failure of the prosecution was largely your fault?"

"Yes."

"Why did you attack the man Dibble?"

Birwitz opened his mouth, but didn't speak. His wife, smouldering until then, caught her breath. Roger shifted his position so that he could see the reflection of the garden in the mirror; and he saw the little brush salesman in one corner of the garden, half hidden by bushes. He did not let the others see that he was taking any notice of anything outside.

He asked: "Did Dibble look as if he were going to pull a gun on you?"

Birwitz didn't answer. Meg said: "That's what happened," in a half-hearted kind of way.

"Birwitz?"

"No," answered Birwitz, heavily. "He didn't move to take any weapon—he didn't have a chance. He had knocked out the uniformed man, and as I thought threatened me with an oar. I just let fly at him."

Roger said: "Knowing he was helpless?"

"Witz," said Meg Birwitz, in a quivering voice, "he trapped you into admitting that."

"All right, Meg."

"If this is how the police work—"

Roger turned to her, and spoke with great deliberation.

"Mrs. Birwitz, I am a senior officer at New Scotland Yard. With my colleagues I have to bear the brunt of all scurrilous attacks made upon the Force—attacks like those made in most of the newspapers this morning. I have to work against heavy odds, and in great difficulty, often because here and there a man on the Force takes bribes, or falls down on his job in some way or other. If you think working against crime is a sinecure, you'll never get the right perspective. If your husband stays in the Force, if he makes the progress that he should do, if he earns promotion until he's posted to the Yard, or to one of the big Divisions as a senior officer, you're going to have a lean time. You're going to know what it is to be left alone for nights on end, never to be sure when he'll come in, never to be sure when he's really safe. You're going to live with a man who's also living with his job, who can't ignore it for any part of the night or day, who can never be sure of getting a complete rest from it. It takes a certain kind of man to handle that particular job, and it takes a certain kind of woman to do her share in it. I think she's got the worst part. I'm sure my wife has. In the first ten or fifteen years of our marriage, we came near to breaking point a dozen times, because she could hardly stand the strain. But she didn't crack under it. Sometimes I look back and wonder how she stood it, but she did. I don't ask to be happier at home than I am."

He stopped. There was a long silence, while the woman stared at him, open-mouthed, all sign of anger vanished.

Birwitz moved to her.

"All right, Meg," he said again.

She didn't speak, just kept staring at Roger.

"Now, let's get on, and let's get one thing clear," said Roger. "I think it's possible that the poison-pen letters had something to do with the case against Mrs. Haughton. I'm a long way from sure, but I think they might have been intended to weaken your morale as a policeman, Birwitz—perhaps to soften you up for taking bribes, perhaps simply to make sure that whenever they wanted an acquittal in the Richmond Court, they had a chance if you were the main police witness. Remember, at the moment I'm guessing—but can you think of any other reason why anyone should want to break up your marriage?"

Birwitz said: "None at all, sir."

"No," said Meg, in a strangled voice. "No."

"Good. Now, the beating-up of Dibble—what was the real reason for it?"

"I just saw red. I suppose—" Birwitz hesitated, then squared his shoulders, giving the impression that he wanted to bring everything into the open. "I suppose I saw him as the man my wife had been out with. I just lost my self-control."

Meg Birwitz moved from his side, and went to the window, staring out; Roger could see no sign of the brush salesman, and he did not look at the woman.

"I'm not a Committee of Inquiry," he pointed out. "I'm not here to get admissions out of you, either. I'm here because I want to find out whether you are in fact being softened up to be a bad policeman—the kind of copper who will take bribes and slant his evidence, who will turn a blind eye to certain crimes. At the moment, you're under suspicion, obviously because you're considered unreliable. If you go back on duty, you might be offered bribery by someone who's on the look-out for corruptible coppers." Roger paused; he heard the rustle of movement as Meg Birwitz turned round, saw the glint in Birwitz's eyes. "If you go back, and attempts are made to bribe you," he repeated, with great deliberation, "you may be able to help the Yard and the whole Metropolitan Police Force, but you'll almost certainly have a nasty time while you're doing it. Some of the newspapers will hold you up as an example of the kind of man we don't want in the Force, and some men at your station won't fancy having you around. You could become unpopular. You might be just the man needed for this particular job."

"What job?" Meg demanded, huskily.

"If your husband is offered bribes for passing on information, I'd like him to accept," said Roger. "The purpose would be to help us find out who is handing out bribes."

"You mean there's a lot of bribery taking place?" asked Birwitz flatly.

"There's no proof, but we think there might be," Roger replied. "We have to find out in a hurry."

After a long pause, Meg said:

"I don't see why anyone should approach my husband. I really don't. Do you, Witz?"

Birwitz said: "I think I ought to know more about it, Mr. West."

"I can't go much further," Roger said. "I can tell you that we know of several instances of lower ranks being approached at times when their resistance was low—like yours is now. The letters you received might have been a softening-up process. Your suspension could easily give you a chip on your shoulder. Even if you're reinstated until the official Inquiry, you'll still have reason for having that chip. That's why I think you might be approached."

"By *whom*?" demanded Birwitz.

"If we knew, I wouldn't be asking you to help," said Roger. "If I'm wrong, we're no worse off. If I'm right, you might soon be able to tell us who it is. That's why I want you to do it."

"Is this—dangerous?" demanded Meg.

"It could be, very," Roger answered. "Let me know as soon as you've made up your mind, Birwitz."

9

THE MAN WHO SOLD BRUSHES

ROGER returned to the local station in time for the luncheon date, after all. Nunn, anxious to be hospitable, and as anxious to know exactly what Roger was up to, offered wine with the roast beef and Yorkshire, cauliflower and oven-baked potatoes, at an inn where the centuries seemed held back by massive oak beams.

"Beer for me, thanks," Roger said. They were in a window seat, safe from being overheard provided they kept their voices down. "The long and short of it is that I think we might use Birwitz to help us find out what's going on. He's taking the day to consider the proposition—that he comes back on duty outwardly on sufferance, to see whether anyone makes an approach to him."

"I see," said Nunn, breaking a piece of bread and smearing farmhouse butter over it. "Well, you know what you're about if anyone does. Mind you, this job proves that Birwitz's got a breaking point. Wouldn't like to put too much reliance in him."

"I won't," Roger said.

"Er—Handsome."

"Yes?"

"This a case by itself, or—?"

"I can't fool you, and I don't want to lie to you," said Roger. "I'm under orders not to give anyone the whole story, but I can go part of the way." Nunn looked smug. "There have been one or two other puzzling cases, and I'm trying to find out if they're connected. Keep it under your hat."

"It's there already," Nunn assured him. "I wondered especially about this brush salesman chap."

"What's new about him?"

"He was in the neighbourhood yesterday, and the day before," said Nunn. "But that isn't unusual—these door-to-door chaps often concentrate on a district for a few days at a time. He works for *Zipp Brushes*, on a commission only—pretty high commission as far as I can gather. We had him checked yesterday, because that kind of street trader might be finding out which houses are easiest to break into—that's how I come to know so much. According to his firm, he picks up as much as fifteen pounds a week on the job."

"Not bad," remarked Roger.

"There's no doubt he was very interested in Birwitz today. I'd say he was watching the house when you arrived, and went along to see what he could find out," Nunn went on. "Must have had a grandstand view of what happened, although he couldn't have heard anything."

"Where did he go?"

"Straight to Richmond Station, where he telephoned a number in the London area—put in his coppers and dialled straight away. The chap I had watching couldn't get the number but he says there were two little numbers in it—o, 1 or 2. He saw that much when the brush salesman dialled."

"What's the salesman's name?"

"Green—Horace Green. I can't tell you much more about him yet. I don't even know where he lives. I didn't want to make *Zipp Brushes* think we'd got anything on him."

"Good thought," said Roger. "Thanks. Where is Green now?"

"He caught a train to Waterloo. I had him followed, and told my chap—young Simpson—to report to me, or to you, whichever was most convenient."

"Couldn't be better," said Roger, as if he meant it. Then he saw the trolley being pushed towards their table. The great silver lid was lifted from a huge joint of beef. "Roast rib," he remarked, almost reverently. "I'd like some of that outside fat, please, and the lean well done."

After lunch, Nunn asked:

"Want me to do anything with Birwitz?"

"He'll let you know if he wants to see me again," said Roger. "Do you think he's really tough enough to stand up to this?"

"Damn' fool question," said Nunn. "We're going to find out. Anything else in mind?"

"Only odds and ends," Roger said.

In fact, the one thing he intended to do, quickly, was to have a C.I.D. man take a job with *Zipp*. He pondered over the right man to send, and finally, he decided on a youthful looking detective sergeant, named Radlett, recently transferred from a fringe division, and not known in Central London. Radlett was one of the breezy, sportsman-car-crazy kind, the perfect type for canvassing door-to-door.

When Roger told him what he was to do, Radlett's brown eyes lit up.

"Just up my street," he declared. "I'll sell so many brushes I'll be leaving the Force to make a fortune, sir."

Roger chuckled, when he had gone out of the office.

"Cheeky young pup," Cope growled, "but he'll do."

*　　*　　*　　*　　*

About the time that Roger and Nunn left the riverside hostelry, in Nunn's car, the little man named Horace Green was walking along Dean Street, Soho, carrying his case of samples. The wind seemed even fiercer than it had during the morning. Metal signs were swinging and clattering. Girls were holding down skirts which hardly covered their knees, anyhow. Dust and litter were eddying about shop doorways.

Green walked with his head down, almost as if he did not want to be recognised.

Detective Constable Simpson felt rather conspicuous, but did not see what else he could do but follow. He did not know whether Green realised that he had been followed; he could only do the job as well as he could, and hope for the best. He had not yet had a chance of reporting back to Richmond, but that did not greatly worry him.

Green turned into a tobacconist's shop.

Simpson saw that from the other side of the road, and immediately entered a newsagent's shop on his side, and bought an *Evening News*. When he stepped outside again, he stood reading the paper, and watching the other shop. Green was there only for a minute or two, but there was a noticeable thing when he came out: he no longer carried his case of samples. He walked with his head lowered, and put on more pace, but Simpson was long-legged, and had no difficulty in keeping up with him.

Simpson saw his quarry turn into Wardour Street, and suspected that Green put on a burst of speed. Did he realise that he was being followed? Simpson quickened his pace, too, but as he stepped into the road a motor-scooter roared towards him. He darted back on to the pavement. The rider called: *"Crazy fool!"* and scorched past. Simpson kicked his left heel against the kerb, and staggered. As he did so, a big, ripe-looking, heavily made-up woman knocked against him. It was like being bumped by a tank. Already off his balance, Simpson went sprawling, while the woman exclaimed shrilly:

"Why don't you look where you're going? Nearly knocked me over, you clumsy lout."

Then she seemed to see the funny side of the complaint, and stood grinning down at Simpson. Two or three people stopped momentarily, but soon hurried on. Simpson picked himself up, smarting from a bruised knee and from anger at having lost his quarry; for there was no sign of Green. He could not be sure that the woman had played a deliberate part in what had

happened, but felt sure that the motor-scooter rider had.
He would recognise the man again, but doubted if the
Superintendent would think it worth asking the Yard
to search for him. What charge could they bring, even
if they found him?

Simpson felt glum about his failure, especially because he knew that he had let the Division down in the
eyes of the Yard.

He went to the nearest telephone kiosk, and reported.

"Stay in that district," Nunn ordered, without hesitation. "I'll arrange for one of the Yard men to contact
you, so that you can describe that scooter rider and the
woman. Keep your eyes open in case you see them
again."

Simpson was surprised but relieved; it was like having
a second chance. The one thing he wanted, above all
others, was to see the man Green again. The next time,
he wouldn't let him go.

* * * * *

Horace Green had realised that he was being followed from the time he had reached Waterloo, and he
had carried out standing instructions carefully; had
gone by bus to Piccadilly Circus, then walked to Dean
Street, and eventually to Wardour Street. Instead of
going to _Zipp_'s offices, he had reported to the manager
by telephone, sure that plans to deal with his follower
would be made quickly.

He had slipped up in one way only, and that had
nothing to do with his instructions. He had left his case
of sample brushes at the tobacconist's, and had been so
preoccupied after telephoning that he had not realised
what he had done until he was nearly home. He told
himself that it would not matter; he could pick it up
in the morning. He was on edge, for he did not know
what job he was working on, although he had an uneasy
feeling that it might be concerned with the shooting of
the policeman.

Green was a caseman for several of the 'Big Boys'. He visited house after house in the residential sections of London's suburbs, checking the quality of furniture, décor, and general prosperity, and then advising the 'Big Boys' whether they were worth a visit. Over the years he had come to judge such conditions to perfection, and seldom recommended a raid without its proving profitable.

It was remarkable how freely housewives and servants talked to a complete stranger. Green had a pleasant manner, and somehow managed to make women feel sorry for him. He looked nearer thirty than forty, although he was forty-five.

The job with *Zipp* was reasonably good, but it was the casing which put him in the money, and had given him the one thing he had never believed he could obtain: his wife.

Out on his rounds, whether on a legitimate sales errand or not, he often dreamed about Betty, knowing that it was his money and all the things he could give her which had won her for him. Certainly it wasn't his looks; he was rather like a rabbit. In actual fact, his face was partly responsible; Betty, like those other woman, had always felt a little sorry for him, and liked him.

She was eighteen.

She was pretty, but not by any means beautiful. He always carried her photograph—in colour, for the most marvellous thing about her was her complexion; it was absolutely smooth, peach-pink, perfect. Her eyes were beautiful, too, and her features small—well, pretty was the word; pretty as a picture. Although she had danced in one of Widderman's clubs, she wasn't a particularly shapely young woman, nice enough, but not bursting out anywhere, and with no remarkable curves. There were times when he looked at her, in the bath, or when she was lying in bed waiting for him, when he felt that she was almost too young to possess.

But she was not; she could stir to passion and be stirred. After his years of loneliness, Horace Green had become as happy as a man could be.

He had been working for the 'Big Boys' for so long that he had almost forgotten there could be any danger in the work. As far as he was aware, Betty knew nothing about his secondary occupation. She didn't ask him where he got his money, and he let her assume that he earned it all from the brushes.

Today, he was worried.

He hadn't wanted to go back to the Richmond area; experience, and the misfortune of other casemen, had taught him the risk of returning to any particular district too often. But the money he received was too good to turn away, and after a mild protest he had broken his self-imposed rule. He had gone back to Hillbrick Avenue, and watched the house where Birwitz lived, to report on anyone who called, and also to case the house. The fact that it was Birwitz's place had been some relief, because that detective had had nothing to do with the shooting. On the other hand, everyone knew what could happen if Birwitz cut loose. Green had done everything he had to, guessing that Birwitz was being cased to see if he would take a drop. When he had left, he had realised he was being tailed by a tall, bony man.

Now Green was free of his tailer, and heading for home, breathing more easily than he had all day; the 'Big Boys' had promised that he would have nothing to worry about, and they'd kept their word. He was in good spirits when he reached Dane Court, in Whitechapel.

This was an area which had been devastated by bombing, years ago, and several new blocks of flats had been put up, with a few small, semi-detached houses. He had bought one of these houses and installed Betty. The fact that she did little or no housework did not trouble him at all. She got him off in the mornings, whenever she was up, and they would usually go out for supper, or have something cold, or a couple of boiled eggs. He was thoroughly content to do the washing-up, while she did the drying. He didn't want her to slave for him, he was so happy with her.

When he reached 11, Dane Court, it was nearly five o'clock. Everything was normal from the outside, and it did not occur to Green that anything was wrong until he had stepped inside the narrow hall, closed the door behind him, and called out:

"I'm back, Betty! Got home early today.'

There was no answer.

That puzzled more than troubled him. Green knew Betty liked to laze indoors in the afternoons, and absolutely hated the wind; he could seldom get her out of doors on a blustery day. He did not call out again, but took off his hat and coat and hung them on a hook near the front door, took out his cigarettes, walked towards the kitchen and said aloud:

"Couldn't I do with a cuppa!"

The door was ajar. Without a second thought, he pushed it open wider, and it banged back almost into his face. At the same time, he saw a small man standing close to the wall on the right of the doorway, but what was far, a thousand times worse, there was Betty.

Betty!

She was wearing her white panties and a pink brassière. She was standing up against the back door, her arms outstretched above her head. In that first, awful glimpse, Green saw that her wrists were tied together, and that the rope round them was hooked over the clothes peg behind the door; she had to stand almost on tip-toe to ease the strain on her arms. She was terrified. Her eyes told him that. Those beautiful brown eyes seemed ablaze with terror. Nothing else could tell him, for her lips were sealed with a patch of sticking plaster, which covered her mouth, leaving her nose and little pointed chin free.

"Come in, Horace," invited that man on the right, as

a second man appeared from behind the door. "Don't shout, don't do anything silly, or someone will get hurt. Just come in and close the door."

10

THREAT

HORACE GREEN's fingers seemed frozen to the door handle. He heard the words but did not take them in. He stared at his wife's slim, girl-like figure, saw the way she was stretched upwards; the slender arching of her waist, the slight distortion of her navel. And again he saw the horror in her eyes.

The man on Green's right repeated roughly: "Come in and close the door."

Green's hand moved slowly from the handle, but he did not step further into the room. The man who had given the orders took two strides forward, and slapped him across the face. Green continued to stare at his wife. He took no more notice of the blow than if he had been brushed by a fly, but his lips began to work.

"I told you—" began the man who had struck him, and grabbed at his right wrist, twisting viciously. Green was propelled forward towards Betty, but came up against a table. The man slammed the door, and rasped: "If you know what's good for you and for her, you'll do what you're told."

"Betty," said Green, chokingly. "Betty."

The man from behind the door began to move. He was taller than the other, had a long jaw and thin cheeks, and his eyes were dark and sardonic. He went up to Betty, and slapped her loudly but not vigorously on her tautly-stretched belly.

"That's the girl," he said. "Fancy you recognising her."

Green made a funny gurgling noise in his throat, and

seemed to sway. Then, without giving the men the
slightest warning, he placed both hands on the kitchen
table and thrust it towards the man who had struck
him; on the same instant, he launched himself at the
one who had slapped his wife. This man, grinning,
pranced about with his fists up, as a boxer in the ring,
taunting Green. Terror flared anew in the girl's eyes.
Green was a yard away from her assailant when the man
kicked at his stomach. Quick as a flash, Green dropped
his right hand to the ankle, gripped, and heaved
upwards. The man went flying backwards, smacked
his head against the wall, and began to slide down,
looking stupid, his mouth open, his eyes strangely
rounded.

The smaller man pushed the table out of the way,
dropped his hand to his waist-band, and snatched off a
length of bicycle chain, worn as a belt. He was small-
featured, small-boned, good-looking in a dark-haired,
sallow-skinned way. He held the chain like a whip, and
crouched in front of Green, waiting for the moment to
strike. The taller man was crumpled up on the floor,
but he was conscious, and if Green had looked round
he would have seen that he was beginning to get up.

Green said in a choking voice: "*You swine, you rotten
swine!*" He leapt forward. The other man slashed out
with the bicycle chain. Betty's body twitched. Green
ducked, the chain whined over his head, he thrust both
hands against the man's chest and smashed him back
against the wall behind the door.

The man's head struck the wall with a thud. Green
saw his arms flop, saw the chain fall, heard it clank on
the floor. He swung round. The taller man was coming
at him now, carrying a cosh. Just on Green's right was
a spindly-looking kitchen chair. He snatched this up,
swung, and brought it down on the man's head. The
blow was so swift and powerful that the other had no
chance to defend himself. A leg of the chair caught him
on the cheek below the eye; he squealed with pain,

and backed away, dropping a cosh. Green bent down, picked up the cosh, and brought it down savagely on the side of the other's head; the man slumped into unconsciousness.

Green was breathing hard and hissingly through his nostrils, his lips tightly compressed. He turned towards Betty, muttering her name beneath his breath. Then he moved towards her, gripped her at the waist, hoisted her up so that he could unhook her from the peg, then lowered her gently into his arms. She sagged against him.

"It's all right," he said huskily. "It's all right, honey, it's all right. I'll get some brandy, that'll get the plaster off. It's all right.

He carried her out of the kitchen and into the front room, and laid her on a couch; she was shivering uncontrollably. He hurried into the hall, took her musquash coat off its hanger, hurried back and spread it over her. Then he switched on the electric fire. "You'll be fine," he muttered. "Don't worry, everything will be all right."

He went out, turned towards the small dining-room opposite, then changed his mind and darted back to the kitchen. The man whose head had banged against the wall was coming round, his eyes flickering; the other was still unconscious. Green snatched up a roll of plaster from the dresser, the plaster they had used to gag his wife. He snipped a piece off, slapped it over the unconscious man's mouth, then turned to the other, who was trying to get up.

As Green moved towards him, he cringed back:

"Okay, Greeny, okay. I know when I'm beat." He put his hand up shakily to defend himself. Green didn't speak, just leaned forward and struck the man's hand aside, then cut off another piece of the tape and stuck it across the quivering mouth.

"Get up," he ordered in a hoarse voice. When the man hesitated, he grabbed his wrist, twisted his arm, hauled him to his feet. "If you don't do what I tell you, I'll break your neck!" He thrust the man in front of him, out of the kitchen, into a cupboard beneath the stairs, a dark, dusty hole filled with boxes, cases and brooms. The man staggered and fell. Green closed the door on him, turned the key in the lock, and went back to the kitchen. He dragged the still unconscious man across to the larder, pushed him inside, and turned that key.

When he had finished, he was breathing very hard, but his movements were more controlled; there was less urgency about what he did. He went into the dining-room, took out a bottle of brandy, poured some on his handkerchief, and hurried into the front room. He knelt down in front of his wife and began to soak the adhesive plaster with the brandy, pressing very gently. The bouquet was strong, and acted like a stimulant; he felt better, and Betty's eyes seemed to become clearer. Soon, Green began to pull the plaster off, soaking it afresh whenever it stuck. At last, he pulled it right off, folded it over, and tossed it into the fireplace.

"It—it's all right," he said, and a touch of anxiety showed in his eyes. "It's all right, isn't it?"

There was a tiny globule of blood on Betty's upper lip, the only sign of injury, although the rest of the skin round her mouth was pink and puffy. She nodded, staring at him in a way he had never known before, and began to move her lips.

"Don't try to talk," he urged. "I'll get you some coffee, and—"

"*What about those men?*" Terror sparked in her eyes.

"I've locked them in the cupboard," Green said, re-assuringly. "They're all right. Don't worry about them. Just lie there and I'll get you some coffee."

"All right," she muttered. "Don't—don't be long."

Green glanced back at her from the door, and she was still staring at him in that unfamiliar way. It made him vaguely uneasy, but he did not lose any time. He went to the front door and bolted it, went to the kitchen and put on a kettle, then bolted the back door. He could hear no sign of movement from either of the cupboards. He rinsed his hands and face in cold water at the kitchen sink, then took out instant coffee, and some cream from the refrigerator. He took two cups of coffee into the front room on a tray.

Betty had changed her position; he saw that she had got up and put the fur coat on, and was sitting corner-wise on the couch, facing the door. Her expression was still vaguely disquieting, but that was lessened by her twisted little smile.

"You all right?"

"I—I'm fine."

"I'll look after you," Green said. "Don't worry, I'll look after you. They won't make any more trouble, you needn't worry. If I'd thought—" He broke off, stirring sugar into Betty's coffee, then handed it to her. "Try and drink that while it's hot. Here! I know what it wants." He snatched up the brandy and splashed some into her coffee. "Nectar, that's what it is now," he declared. "Nectar!"

"Horace," Betty said in a funny little voice, "you were wonderful."

He could hardly believe his ears.

"Me? Why, I just—"

"You were absolutely wonderful," Betty choked. "The way you set about *two* of them." She stretched out her arm and put the cup on the table. He thrust his by it, slopping coffee into the saucer. Quite suddenly his arms were round her, and she was hugging him, crying in deep, convulsive sobs. But they did not matter. Nothing mattered for that moment but the wonder of what she had said.

* * * * *

"More coffee?" Green asked.

"Not yet, Horace."

"Feeling okay?"

"I'm fine, now."

"Like to talk to me about it?"

Betty moistened her lips.

"Well, it all happened so quickly," she said. "I was lying down upstairs, having my rest." Green knew that she had almost certainly been watching television and eating chocolates; that was what he encouraged her to do. "There was a sound outside the door. I was ever so frightened at first, but then I thought it was you, playing a joke on me."

Green didn't speak.

"Then—then they rushed in." Betty almost screamed.

"If they hurt—"

"They were a bit rough, but they didn't touch me—you know what I mean," said Betty, unsteadily. "They told me to get off the bed, and made me go downstairs. I—I'd got the room ever so warm, I was just wearing my bra and panties, you always say you like me to have a proper rest in the afternoons, and I stayed up there till late, there was a Western." She paused, as if guiltily, but Green made no comment, and she went on: "So they made me walk downstairs, just like I was, and then told me they wanted to talk to you. They—well you saw what they did, Horace. It was awful."

"I saw all right," he said. "You—you wouldn't fool me, would you? They didn't touch you?"

"I swear it, Horace."

"That's all right," he said. "That's all right, then." He stood up from the chair which he had drawn in front of the couch, and took out cigarettes. "Well, we've got to decide the next thing to do. I'd better go and find out what they wanted to see me about."

"Horace, don't you know?"

"Not for sure, I don't," he said. "But I've got an idea. Betty, you'd better know this, though. I haven't made all the money I get from selling brushes, I—"

"Don't be silly," she interrupted. "Do you think I'm dumb?"

"*What?*"

"I knew you must be doing something on the side."

"And you didn't *care*?"

"Why should I care? I wasn't doing it," retorted Betty simply. Her lips were still flushed, and the globule of blood had smeared and dried, but she looked very young and beguiling with the fur up to her chin, and only her ankles and feet showing beneath the bottom of the coat; she was curled up so comfortably. "What's the sideline, Horace?"

He told her, briefly, and she nodded with grave understanding and even approval. Then he told her what had happened that day, how he had been followed to Soho, how the men he worked for had dealt with the detective from Richmond.

"Now let's see what we've got to do," he said, drawing deeply on the cigarette. "I'll tell you what—you go upstairs and get dressed, while I talk to one of them. They'll talk about right, now. Then when I know what they came for, we can decide what to do. I think you ought to go away for a few days, honey. I don't want—"

"I'll go away if you'll come with me," Betty said. "But don't you run away with the idea that I'm going to leave you on your own while this is going on. My place is by your side, Horace."

"We'll see," said Green. He wanted to hug her, wanted somehow to show her what delight her words gave him. "Come on, you go and get some clothes on, and I'll talk to Caprini."

"Who?"

"Caprini—he's the one who started on me," said Green. "The other one's name is Deemer. I think it'll be a long time before he can talk, but Caprini—he'll come across all right."

"You be careful," Betty urged.

II

CAPRINI TALKS

"So the 'Big Boys' told you to come round here and rough me up," Green said to the little dark-haired man. They were in the kitchen, and Caprini was sitting with his arms resting on the back of a chair—the chair which had been used to hit Deemer. Green had made him push his hands through the slats of the back of the chair, and had tied his wrists together; he was helpless, almost as helpless as Betty had been. He was pale, too, and kept licking his lips; his eyes had lost their boldness.

"That's right," he muttered.

"Who told you to rough my wife up?"

"Listen, we didn't hurt—"

"Just answer the question."

"It—it was Deemer's idea. Deemer said if you came in and saw what we could do to her, you wouldn't take any chances, you'd come to heel quickly."

"Just Deemer, eh?"

"Yeh."

"You didn't have anything to do with it?"

"Dee—Deemer was the boss."

"Listen, Caprini," Green said. "If you or Deemer or anyone else ever lays a finger on my wife again, I'll kill you. Just pass the word around. I'll kill you—I'll kill anyone who touches her." He waited long enough for that to sink in, and then went on: "Which of the 'Big Boys' was it? Rocky?"

"Green, if I squeal—"

"Just think what can happen to you if you don't answer my questions."

Caprini half closed his eyes, and said dismally:

"Yeh, it was Rocky."

"Just Rocky?"

"Yeh."

"What did he tell you to do?"

"He said to come and tell you not to open your trap if the police asked questions. He said you'd been followed from Richmond, and the cops might catch up with you. He just wanted to make sure you didn't open your trap. He said—"

"Tell me."

"He said to tell you that if you squealed, your wife would squeal in a different kind of way."

Green said: "So he did, and you decided to prove it. That was your big mistake. What else?"

"That's the lot, Green, I swear it."

"You just had to tell me not to squeal?"

"That's right, I swear—"

Green said: "Okay, so you swear. I wouldn't trust you if you swore on your own mother's grave, but I've wasted enough time with you. Now I'll tell you what I'm going to do. I'm going to shave your head, and I'm going to shave Deemer's, and I'm going to send you back to Rocky. After you've gone, I'll talk to him on the telephone. Just tell him to be in tonight. If he's not, I'll ask for police protection, and he'll know what that means. Got me?"

"Listen, you don't have to shave my head! You—"

"I want you to remember me for a long time," said Green. "You can tell Rocky another thing while he's waiting for me to telephone. You can tell him that I learned all about fighting when I was in the Army, and if he really wants trouble, he can have it. Now hitch your chair over to the sink."

He did not use soap on their heads; just an electric razor.

*　　*　　*　　*　　*

"Now they've gone, we're going to get a move on," Green said to Betty. "I wouldn't trust them round the corner. We're going up to the West End, we'll stay at the Regent Palace—be as safe there as if we were in Scotland Yard. If Rocky or any of the others try anything, I'll talk to the coppers. You ready?"

"I just want to put on my hat."

"That's okay by me," said Green. "That's perfectly okay by me."

* * * * *

"I want you to know the facts of life, Rocky," Green said into a telephone from the hotel near Piccadilly. "If you or anyone else puts a hand on my wife again, I just lift the receiver and call the Yard. I've got too much on you for you to chance that. You leave me alone, and I'll keep mum. I'll stay in hiding so that the cops can't find me, and if they find me, okay, I'll close up. But if you lay a finger on Betty, you're going right down the drain."

"Greeny, you've got me all wrong," protested the man named Rocky. "I wouldn't dream of touching Betty, she's a nice girl. Deemer and Cap ain't got no sense. You don't have anything to worry about from me, just keep in hiding and away from the cops."

Green didn't answer.

"You hear me, Greeny?"

"I hear you," Green said. "I've told you what I'll do, but I haven't told you how much this job will cost you, Rocky. Two weeks' work, say, at a hundred nicker a week. Just put it in a parcel and address it to Betty Green, care of Piccadilly Post Office."

"Now, listen, Greeny, you can collect the dough any time you like!"

"I'll collect it from the Piccadilly Post Office," said Green. "Tomorrow sometime. Have it there by two o'clock. Don't forget."

Rocky said gruffly: "It'll be there."

"It had better be," said Green, and rang off.

He was smiling, tautly.

He was sitting on one of the twin beds, and looking at Betty, who was lying on the other. She had the sheet pulled up to her chin; she rather liked doing that, as if she realised how desirable and how young it made her seem. Her hair was beautifully waved. Her lips were normal again; only a tiny blemish showed where the globule of blood had been. She had the same expression in her eyes as she had earlier, the expression which had puzzled him; but it did not puzzle him now.

"Okay?"

"*Okay!*" she exclaimed. "Two hundred nicker!"

"Easy money."

"Easy money," Betty echoed, shrilly. "Horace, I didn't think you had it in you."

"Life's full of surprises, eh?"

"Talking to Rocky Marlo like that!"

"So he's Rocky Marlo, a 'Big Boy'. He knows how much I know, and he won't try any more funny stuff. He thought it was a pushover, but he didn't know what happened to me when I married my girl."

"Didn't he, Horace?"

"Listen, hon," said Green, leaning forward so that his face was only a foot away from hers, "There's you and me, and that's all I want. That's my little lot and I'll fight the world for it. I don't want trouble. I won't cause nobody any trouble. If I run into any doing the job I'm paid for, okay, that's part of the risk. If I had to go away for a year or two you'd be all right, I'd see to that—so long as you was waiting for me when I came out, that would be all I'd worry about. But if Rocky or Caprini or Deemer or anyone else starts trouble, they can have it. What do they think I'm a caseman for? I can tell Rocky Marlo things about himself that he's almost forgotten. Don't you worry, Betty."

"Horace," she said, a few seconds later.

"Yes, hon?"

"Supposing they ganged up on you?"

"They won't—not when they've had time to cool off," Green assured her. "The only danger was tonight. After tonight they'll be careful, don't worry."

"I don't trust Caprini."

"You don't have to," said Green, with fervour. "But you don't have to think about him right now, hon. Whatever Rocky says, Caprini will do. And Rocky won't want to take any chances. The time to worry about Caprini and Deemer will be later, when it's all over, but you still won't have to worry. I can look after things. Anybody ever tell you that we've got to spend the rest of our lives in London?"

"Horace!"

Green laughed, excitedly, almost with a touch of hysteria, he was so happy at the way things had gone. He stood up slowly, and slid open his shirt front; as he did so, Betty flung back the sheet which covered her, and lay like a kitten, curled up, seductive, skin as smooth as satin, arms folded across her provocative little breasts.

*   *   *   *   *

The following morning, Friday, Roger West woke to the sound of laughter from along the landing, lay on his back for a few minutes, drowsily, with his wife lying close to him, still sleeping heavily. Her face was half-buried in the pillows, her dark hair with its pattern of grey showed against the white pillow.

The sun was shining, and there seemed to be no wind.

Roger got up, and Janet stirred, but did not wake. He untied and retied the sash of his pyjamas, stepped out of the bedroom in this house in Bell Street, Chelsea, and saw shadowy figures moving on the passage wall. The boys' room faced north-east, the sun was streaming in, and they were obviously sparring. He went along stealthily.

Richard, his younger son, now sixteen, had his back to the door. Martin, called Scoopy, now seventeen, a little shorter but with very broad muscle-packed shoulders, faced the passage. He was weaving and ducking as Richard kept pushing out straight lefts to his face. Martin was laughing; once he started to laugh it took a great deal to stop him.

He saw Roger.

"Hi, Dad!"

"Dad!" Richard swung round. "'Morning!"

"Puffing and blowing like a grampus," said Roger. "When I was your age, I had to keep fit."

"I'll keep you fit," scoffed Scoop, and dropped into a boxing stance. "Come on, let me show you."

Roger said: "Some other time. Pity I was so late last night that I didn't see you. How are tricks?"

"Fine," said Richard.

"As a matter of fact, Dad, I've problems," said Martin, suddenly very earnest. The next words came out with a rush. "It's a question of whether I stay on at school for another three terms, and have a bash at a University Scholarship, or not. Did Mum tell you?" He was very eager. Obviously this had been pent-up inside him; release had come like pressing a button.

"No. She was asleep when I came in," Roger answered, evasively. It was the first time this subject had ever been broached, and he must show some kind of sympathetic reaction without positive approval. "Want to have a bash?"

"Well, it wouldn't do any harm—that's if it doesn't interfere with any of your plans," the lad qualified quickly.

"I don't want to go on to a University," Richard declared. "I'm too thick!" He gave a self-deprecatory smile. "So if I'm out at work earning some cash, it won't be so bad if Scoop goes to a University, will it?"

"Oh, you'll soon earn plenty for all the family," Roger said. "Good old Fish! When do you have to make the decision, Scoop?"

"Not until the beginning of the Summer term, but the Head said the quicker I made up my mind, the better."

"Let's agenda it for the week-end," decided Roger. "Sunday afternoon, say."

"Are you going to be home?"

"I don't see why not, as things are at present," Roger said. "I'll make sure I'm home part of the day, anyhow, and I'll think about it meanwhile. One of you nip down and put a kettle on."

He hoped that he had shown sufficient interest without giving too much encouragement; it needed a lot of thought, as well as discussion with Janet. There certainly wasn't time this morning.

Richard made the tea. Janet was sitting up, but still heavy-eyed, when Roger took it in. She was at an age where it was wise to take things more easily than she wanted. She was always tired at night, almost as tired first thing in the morning. By breakfast time, however, she would be as bright as a cricket. She came down in her dressing-gown to cook breakfast, the boys hanging around and joking with her, while Roger had a shave and a shower.

He stepped out of the Bell Street house a little before half past eight. Richard had already got the car out of the garage, and reversed it to within an inch of the pavement; he wasn't yet old enough for his licence, and was under strict promise not to take it off the drive. He was sitting at the controls, looking as if he wished he were on the race track.

Roger took over, drove towards King's Road, and saw Richard waving and Scoop standing with him.

This university suggestion was one he should have talked about with Janet earlier, and he was vexed with himself. It had often crossed his mind that Martin might like to try for a University scholarship, but there was so much pressure of work that he had never got round to thinking seriously about the pros and cons.

He had a half-guilty feeling, which persisted until he began to think of the Birwitzes, and the answer which he would get this morning. The Birwitzes lived in a rather better yet a similar kind of street to Bell Street; and there was some parallel between the Birwitzes and the Wests, for he and Janet had put off having a child until they felt they could afford it.

Roger turned into the Yard at ten minutes to nine. As he started up the stone steps leading to the C.I.D. building, Martin called Scoopy had receded to the back of his mind.

Cope was in.

"What've we got, Dave?" demanded Roger.

"Nothing much," said Cope, shuffling some papers on his desk. "That brush salesman, Green, has disappeared from home. He and his wife left about seven o'clock, carrying a suitcase."

"On the run, eh," mused Roger. "Call out for them?"

"Yes—to watch, not pull them in."

"That's right."

"Funny story going the rounds in the East End," went on Cope. "Two of Rocky Marlo's boys are said to have been waiting for Green when he got home. They left before the Greens, and turned up at Rocky's place looking like monks."

"Monks?"

"Their heads were shaved, and one of 'em had a hell of a black eye," said Cope, with a broad grin. "I've got feelers out trying to discover what really happened, but the situation we've got to face is that Green's in hiding, after a visit from Rocky's muscle-men. That suggests—"

"We pick up Rocky for questioning," interrupted Roger. "Might be useful, later. We'll wait a bit, I think, but we'll have Rocky and these two men of his closely watched."

"I've laid that on."

"What would we do without you?" jeered Roger. "Thanks, Dave." He tossed his hat towards a peg, missed, bent down to pick it up, and sat on the corner of his desk. "Anything in from Radlett?"

"He's got the job with *Zipp*, three-ten a week plus twenty-five per cent commission on sales, and he's been sent out to the North London area. All the door-to-door salesmen have to report in to Head Office once a day, and there's a kind of sales conference most Saturday mornings."

"That's about right for Radlett," Roger approved. "Now we'll see what he's made of." The sun was shining brightly, and the river looked calm and inviting, as he stared out of the window. "At least he can go around without being blown off his feet today. How about that young solicitor, Cartwright?"

"His firm does act for Mrs. Haughton—has done for years."

"Hmm."

"Mrs. H. doesn't have a typewriter."

Roger looked down his nose. "I'm not doing so well, am I?"

Cope grinned.

"You do all right, guv'nor! I've had reports in from every one of those special cases you wanted checked, and we can't find any evidence of a connection. Did you really expect one?"

"I just hoped," said Roger. He felt suddenly dispirited, for the morning was yielding nothing new or encouraging. He did not ask for news from Birwitz; Cope would have told him had it come through.

He sat at his desk, flipped over reports, saw with some relief that there was nothing special for him to do, and called across to Cope: "I think I'll go and have a talk with Widderman. He's usually at his office between ten and eleven, isn't he?"

"Just like a real businessman! If that man peddled motor cars instead of vice, I could almost respect him. Er—you know there was once a tie-up between him and Rocky Marlo, don't you?"

"Didn't they have a quarrel?"

"Two years ago."

"Thanks," said Roger. "Call me at Widderman's if anything comes through. How's Dibble?"

"Improving."

"That shot policeman—Thompson?"

"He'll be out of hospital for the week-end."

"Celebrations in his family," remarked Roger, and was going towards the door when a telephone bell rang. Cope got up, leaned across, and answered it.

He glanced up.

"It's Nunn, from Richmond," he said.

*   *   *   *   *

"I've just had a word with Birwitz," Nunn told Roger, "and he would like to go along with you. I've told him to be ready to report for duty again on Monday morning. Is that all right?"

"Yes," said Roger. "That's fine. I'll want to see him again before he starts, but we can fix that later."

When he left the Yard, he was in higher spirits, and looking forward to his interview with Widderman, the man who should surely have been found guilty of gaming, but had got off because of poorly delivered evidence.

12

WIDDERMAN

WIDDERMAN owned a lot of property in the Soho district, owned and operated three of the new kind of strip-tease night clubs, and was believed to be the organising mind behind a great deal of the prostitution and the vice in the West End of London. As Roger went up to his office in a tiny lift which had just room beside for a small youth, and which crawled upwards, Roger thought of what Cope had said: put Widderman in a different business, and he would be likeable, or at least a man to respect.

The lift stopped at a small passage, with one room leading off it, marked: *Saul Widderman, Private*. The youth tapped and a woman called "Come in." The youth opened the door and Roger stepped into a small but well-furnished office, where a woman sat at a type-writer on a desk placed slantwise by a small window, so that the light fell on her machine and papers. She was in her middle-thirties, pleasant-looking, made-up well but not by any means extravagantly. She wore a knitted two-piece of a brick-red colour, and a dark green skirt. She smiled, rather aloofly.

"Mr. West?"

"Yes."

"I'm Muriel Kennedy, Mr. Widderman's secretary." She paused, as if expecting Roger to make some comment beyond: "How are you?" He didn't. The name Kennedy rung a bell, but he couldn't identify it at the moment. The woman went on: "Mr. Widderman won't keep you more than three or four minutes."

"Thank you." Roger wanted to stare; there was something familiar about her. He couldn't make out what it was, and that annoyed him. His memory shouldn't play him this kind of trick. Had Muriel Kennedy worked for an ordinary business man, she would have seemed absolutely in keeping; somehow it was hard to associate her with a man of Widderman's reputation.

Muriel Kennedy—*Kennedy!*

The bell rang clearly, even resoundingly—both the name and the likeness between two people had made him remember. This was the daughter of ex-Chief Inspector Kennedy of the C.I.D., that one-time friend of the Assistant Commissioner, who had been dismissed from the Force, and had served twelve months in prison, for taking bribes from a fence. The likeness seemed unmistakable now; Kennedy had been a good-looking man.

He was still.

The woman was smiling, a little less coldly.

"Have you placed me, Mr. West?"

"I think so."

"My father and I were talking about you only the other evening," she said.

"Really?"

"He was saying that he always believed you would go a long way," declared Muriel Kennedy.

Roger laughed. "I wouldn't have expected him to remember me."

"I don't think there is very much that my father forgets," retorted Muriel Kennedy. A buzzer sounded on her desk, and she stood up. "That's Mr. Widderman now." She passed Roger and opened the door. "Super-intendent West," she announced. Roger had a feeling that she was laughing at him—in the kind of way that Widderman must be laughing, and Mrs. Haughton, and the others who should have been convicted of some crime, but had managed to escape.

Widderman was standing up behind a large desk in an unexpectedly large room, panelled in walnut, which had heavy curtains with deep pelmets, two comfortable modern armchairs, and several oil paintings of women, all of them cabaret or night club stars. On a filing cabinet at his side was, also unexpectedly, a photograph of Muriel Kennedy in a cocktail dress: she looked distinguished and quite lovely.

"Come and sit down," Widderman said; he did not offer to shake hands. "May I send for some coffee?"

"Not for me, thanks."

"Very well." Widderman glanced at the woman. "All right, Muriel, thank you. Make sure we're not disturbed, won't you?"

"Yes, of course." The door closed.

Widderman sat down, and pushed cigarettes across his desk. The air of opulence was unmistakable, but there was a great deal of taste in this room, too. Widderman himself was a rather short stocky man with a broad face and broad features. His hair was thick and grey; it curled a little, attractively. There was something of the boxer about him; Roger saw a certain vague likeness to Jack Dempsey. He wore a suit of medium grey, beautifully cut. His starched collar and cuffs, his tie and tie-pin, were all exactly right. This man might have stepped out of the *Tailor and Cutter*.

"I've been trying to imagine what you might want," he said. "If I can help, I'll be glad to."

Roger said: "Thanks." He paused, then asked: "How did you get at the police witness yesterday?"

Widderman's expression didn't really change; yet a hint of a smile crept into his grey eyes, as if he were mildly amused, and even slightly derisive.

"I didn't get at him."

Roger said: "He told one story to us at the Yard, and allowed your solicitor to force him to change it."

"I thought the solicitor was a very smart young man," Widderman said. "I was very pleased with him, and he and his firm can rely on a good share of my work in future."

"I can imagine that," said Roger, drily. He settled himself more comfortably in his chair. "It won't surprise you to know that we think our man was bribed."

"Indeed?"

"And it won't surprise you to know that we intend to find out whether that's true, and, if so, who was behind it."

"I'm sure you want to," said Widderman. He spread his hands on his desk, palms downwards. The nails were manicured, the fingers a pale white; the hands of a man who did not know the meaning of manual work. His voice was quiet, cultured, pleasing. The fact that he was Jewish was hardly evident in his

appearance and certainly not in his manner. "Let me
try to save you some trouble, Mr. West. I did not bribe
or attempt to bribe your witness, and to my knowledge
my solicitor did not, either. I have a great deal of
wholly legitimate business—business which you may
not approve, but which is quite legal and very profitable. I would not take the risk of being caught attempt-
ing to corrupt the police—except, of course, corrupting
the morals of any policemen who visit my clubs!"

It would be easy to laugh with him.

Roger said: "The case is over, you've nothing at all
to fear from it now. Were you on the premises at the
time of the police raid?"

"Yes," answered Widderman, and his smile grew
broader. "I took no part in the gaming, but I knew it
was going on. I let off that particular apartment
privately, and cannot be held responsible for the
behaviour of my tenants, but I was in a highly vulner-
able position."

"Did you expect to be found guilty?"

"I was afraid I would be, and very relieved when I
wasn't."

"Yet you allowed a young and inexperienced solicitor
to appear for you."

"Yes, I did." said Widderman. "My usual man,
Lieber, is away, and he recommended this young man
very warmly. I had no reason to believe that a lawyer
could affect the verdict here. The case seemed quite
straightforward. I hoped to get off with a fine, but I
knew there was a risk of a short prison sentence, as no
doubt you hoped."

He broke off, still with that faint smile.

Roger had a feeling that he was speaking the truth.
He was too frank, too dispassionate, to be lying. And
the key point of this visit was not to catch Widderman
out on any of his past offences, but to find out if he had
been behind the bribing of the Yard man.

Supposing the man hadn't been bribed.

Supposing it was a case, like Birwitz's, of a man being under considerable emotional pressure?

"Have you any other questions?" Widderman asked.

Roger said: "Yes. Are any of these names familiar? For a start, Birwitz?"

Widderman actually chuckled.

"He's surely quite notorious."

"Mrs. Haughton."

Widderman frowned. "No, I don't think so."

"Cartwright?"

Widderman said: "I know an old man named Septimus Cartwright, but I can't believe he is the man you mean. You sent him to jail some years ago, and he's been out for about six months."

"Not that Cartwright," agreed Roger. "Green—Horace Green."

Widderman echoed, quietly: "Horace Green, a man who sells brushes. Is that the one?"

"Yes."

"I know him very slightly. He married a nice little girl who danced in one of my floor shows, and persuaded her to stop working."

"Have you heard of him this week?"

"No."

"Or from his wife?"

"No."

"Rocky Marlo?"

Widderman said: "You are well aware that I know Marlo. He was once a partner in some of my businesses, and I broke the association for a reason you will find it difficult to believe."

"Try me," invited Roger.

"He kept trying to turn my clubs into thieves' dens," Widderman said, very clearly. "He organised pickpockets of both sexes, and took a cut in anything they stole. West, let me make one thing clear. I don't agree with you, or with the authorities, on what constitutes vice. If a man comes to one of my clubs, and cares to

go off and sleep with one of the girls, and if the girl
has no objection, that is all right with me. If it is a
financial transaction between the man and the girl,
that's still all right with me, but I don't want any share
in it. I know that you at the Yard think I organise it,
and take a cut, but you're wrong. Rocky Marlo started
to organise that kind of racket. He used to terrorise the
girls into robbing anyone who slept with them, and he
took his cut of that also. As soon as I found out, I
broke the partnership. Do you remember when two of
my clubs were raided by a gang of hooligans?"

"Yes."

"That was Marlo's form of revenge."

"Why didn't he go on taking revenge?"

Widderman said: "I bought him off, for one thing,
and I told him I'd inform the police, for another. That
threat stopped him in his tracks. Why did you mention
Marlo?"

"Was Green one of his runners?"

Widderman said: "It's no part of my business to talk
about Green."

"Would Marlo have any reason for working on
Green?"

"I don't know," said Widderman, as if this line of
questioning puzzled him. "Marlo has a lot of irons in
the fire. He organises different kinds of crimes, as you
know quite well. Up to a point, he's a clever operator,
and he certainly makes a lot of money. But he doesn't
work with or for me, Mr. West, and he is never likely to."

Roger said: "Supposing I told you that Marlo was
behind the man Cotten, whose evidence against you
fell down in court—would you believe it?"

"No, I would not," said Widderman. "Marlo would
do a lot to see me inside prison, and wouldn't lift a
finger to keep me out of it. Mr. West, while you're here
I'd like to make one thing clear. In general, I do not
break the law. I might be caught out in some indis-
cretion, as with the gaming the other night, but most

of my activities can stand up to the closest police examination. I may sail close to the wind, but I do not break the law for profit. To make sure of that, I keep the most astute solicitor in London on my retainer list, as you know. You may not know that I also have a consultant who can see everything from the point of view of the police as well as from my own angle. You met his daughter outside. You will be wasting your time if you try to break me. I can't be broken. And what is more, I don't do anything that shames me or need worry anybody. Supposing you get that clear."

13

ROCKY MARLO

ROGER leaned back in his chair and looked at the man, without speaking. Widderman sat with his hands flat on his desk: broad, handsome, immaculate, apparently quite sure of himself. Roger had a sense of crisis; that he could handle this situation in a way which could lead to confusion and ill feeling, or that he could handle it so as to make a friend of Widderman. 'Friend' was an odd word to think in these circumstances.

Widderman was more on edge than he made out; and he broke the silence.

"Or are your prejudices too strong, Mr. West?" That offered a note of challenge and of resentment.

Roger gave a quick, bright grin.

"When I work on prejudice, I always get a kick in the pants afterwards," he said. "But my information is pretty positive."

"What information?"

"About you."

Widderman said: "Supposing you tell me what it is."

"I'm going to," said Roger. By forcing the pace, he

was deliberately trying to change the mood, and he believed that Widderman was puzzled. He leaned forward: "Shall we record it all on the tape recorder on your desk, so that it goes down to posterity?" He had not expected Widderman to flush; but the man did, and his eyes looked very bright because of it.

Roger laughed.

"As we're getting things straight, let's make a job of it," he said. "The use of a tape recorder to keep a record of this kind of conversation is quite normal. The police can't use the method often, because it isn't regarded as playing fair, but any crook, whether he's a millionaire or Rocky Marlo, can use it—or can use any dirty, lying trick to get the better of the police and the better of society."

"Now, West—"

"My turn to talk," interrupted Roger. He spread his hands on the desk and leaned forward so that he could almost touch Widderman's hands. "Whether you like it or not, you've a bad reputation at Scotland Yard and in Fleet Street—so bad that it stinks. You say you don't deserve it. You say you broke with Marlo because he wasn't playing straight, that it was Marlo who earned the reputation for the depths of degradation, for organising vice and living on the proceeds. Well, that isn't what we believe at the Yard. We think that you quarrelled with Marlo because you couldn't agree on how to divide the profits made out of this filth. We think it was a case of vice kings falling out. Can you prove that it wasn't?"

Widderman was now a dusky red; with anger?

"Can you?" repeated Roger. "Or do you expect me to go away believing that you're the white-headed boy who wouldn't do any little Mummy's girl a moment's harm? Because I won't—unless I get a lot more evidence. I shall go out believing that you live and grow fat on vice, that no young girl who comes into your clutches is likely to get out clean, that you organise and

make profit out of vice, perversion, the sex-obsession
of fools, and—"

"That's enough, West!"

"I'm telling you about your reputation."

"I won't have—"

"Listen to me," said Roger, roughly. "You may think
I'm insulting you, but in fact I'm doing you a big
favour. I'm telling you what we think of you, and I'm
warning you that if we're right we'll come after you
with everything we've got. If we're wrong, if you don't
deserve this reputation, give me some proof. Give me
something I can take back to the Assistant Commissioner and say: 'I think we ought to lay off Widderman,
he's not so black as he's painted.' Because we've got
plenty to do," Roger went on, almost savagely. "We've
got more than our hands full, and you know it. If we
caught every trafficker in vice in London, we still
wouldn't be half-way out of trouble. We'd still have a
thousand nasty little beasts and a thousand vicious little
crooks in this area alone, and there are plenty more
crimes in the rest of London. You know as well as I do
that we're seriously undermanned. We can't patrol the
streets as we'd like to—if we put a big force on to one
job, we have to take men off another. We've got it
tough, Widderman, and we don't want to waste a
minute or a man. So if we can stop working on you,
that's what we'd like. I could hand you out the line
that we don't want to prosecute innocent men, but I'm
telling you face to face—we don't want to waste our
time on men who are only on the fringes of the business.
Now—where's that proof?"

Widderman's cheeks were back to their normal colour.
His eyes were narrowed, bright, but no longer angry.
He moved back in his chair, and asked:

"What kind of proof do you want? You can examine
the books of all my clubs—each one is a different company. You can see my bank statements, and my security
lists. You can—"

"Thanks," said Roger, and felt suddenly much more cheerful. He had made a break through, of a kind, and it seemed more than ever likely that Widderman was telling the truth. "I'll be satisfied with just one proved fact," he went on.

"Name it!"

"Proof that you quarrelled with Marlo for the reasons you've given. If you can convince me of that, I'll know where I am."

Widderman hesitated, drummed the desk with his fingers for a few moments, then pressed a bell-push. The door behind Roger opened on the instant, and Muriel Kennedy said:

"Yes, Saul?"

"Have you heard all of this?"

"Yes," the woman answered. Roger glanced round at her and got the impression that she had not recovered from anger as quickly as Widderman. She looked at him without any of the friendliness with which she had greeted him.

"Have you got the Marlo tapes handy?" Widderman asked.

"It will take me five minutes to get them."

"I fancy that Mr. West will wait," said Widderman.

* * * * *

The record of the conversation between Widderman and Marlo came off the tape perfectly. The contrast was striking between Widderman's cultured voice, never hurried, never flurried, and Marlo's hard, angry tone, with its overtone of Cockney.

There could have been no more revealing conversation. Everything that Widderman had claimed seemed to be true: he accused Marlo of living on girls, of using his, Widderman's clubs to get his hands on his victims, of every kind of vice and crime that thrived in Soho. The longer it went on, the louder Marlo shouted. Then he began to bluster.

"I don't think you will be well advised to do anything to me, or to Muriel, or to my clubs," Widderman told him. "I have other tapes, which would be enough to send you down for ten years. I have a lot more evidence against you. We're through, Marlo. You can take exactly the amount due to you, and after that keep away from me. Is that clear?"

"I'll see you dead first," Marlo growled.

*   *   *   *   *

Widderman switched off the recorder, and the voices died away. Muriel Kennedy was sitting on an upright chair, in a corner of the office, more relaxed now, looking at Roger as if to say: 'How wrong can you be?'

Widderman pushed his chair back from the desk, and said:

"He wrecked two of my smaller clubs, but I took no action—I expected a man of Marlo's temperament to let off steam. He didn't in fact do much damage, except to a few pieces of furniture. We weren't forced to close even for one night. And since then I've had no trouble with him."

Roger said: "That's good. And you have no dealings with him at all?"

"None."

"Do his men frequent your clubs?"

"Probably," replied Widderman. He spread his hands. "I can't be sure who is on his payroll and who isn't. They change from time to time. I intend to keep my clubs open to anybody who is prepared to pay and to behave himself, and who simply wants to see a few naked girls dancing, or a few mildly salacious scenes. Scenes which really do no harm, Mr. West." He glanced at Muriel. "Don't you agree?"

"If Mr. West was as good as he thinks he is, he would have had reports from the clubs to convince him of that."

"You see, Mr. West," Widderman murmured.

"I see," said Roger.

"Aren't you satisfied now?" demanded the woman.

Roger stood up slowly, moved towards the door, leaned on the wall near it, and said with great deliberation:

"I'm as nearly convinced as I'm ever likely to be. But there's one thing you've forgotten."

"What is it?" asked Widderman, sharply.

Muriel Kennedy said under her breath: "So he was right." She turned away, reminding Roger of Meg Birwitz, unable to find words, turning her back on him and her husband.

"We don't make up these stories," Roger said. "There's been a steady stream of circumstantial evidence and of hearsay that you are what we thought you were. When we pick up a pimp, he's likely to ask us why we don't go for you, the Boss, instead of picking on him. At least two disorderly houses are in property owned by you or one or two of your associates. We—"

"Listen to me, Mr. West," Widderman interrupted. "I don't want there to be any mistake at all about this. The oldest profession in the world hasn't been prospering for so long because it's vicious or unnatural. I wouldn't want a daughter of mine to become a prostitute, but these girls have their uses, and they're human beings. If they pay a fair rent and keep my premises in reasonable condition, I'm not going to turn them out. You're a policeman, and your job's with the law, not with any particular conception of morals."

Roger smiled faintly. "I couldn't agree with you more." He looked at Muriel Kennedy. "Are they your sentiments too, Miss Kennedy?"

She turned to face him.

"I accept life as it is. Are you or are you not going to stop persecuting Mr. Widderman?"

"We're going to stop," Roger said, "unless we're forced to continue."

"Oh, more double talk!" Bitterness rang deep in the woman's voice.

"If we get information lodged against Mr. Widderman, or if we get evidence against him of any crime, we'll take action," Roger went on. "We certainly won't go all out to get him on the strength of what I've heard today, but *someone* is going all out."

"I don't understand you," Widderman said. Muriel Kennedy raised her hands and declared:

"He's simply twisting the situation round, Saul. Why don't you show him the door?"

"Go on, Mr. West," said Widderman.

"Someone is gunning for you," Roger declared earnestly. "Someone spreads this evidence and this talk. It was a squeak from an informer which put us on to the raid the night before last. Someone is gunning for you all the time, and they're doing it through us. Do you know who it is?"

"I don't believe it," Muriel said.

"Do you, Mr. Widderman?"

"I suppose it could be true," said Widderman slowly. "And I suppose it could be Marlo."

"There's one thing you can do to help get the situation quite clear," said Roger.

"What is it?"

"If it's Marlo, if you get proof that it is, let me know."

"I most certainly will."

"Thanks," said Roger. He turned towards the door, and the woman moved to open it; she still had an angry hostile look. As she opened the door, Roger said: "So we haven't changed, Miss Kennedy?"

"You certainly haven't."

"From when?"

"From the days when you drummed my father out of the police force."

"Ah," said Roger. "Does it still hurt him?"

She didn't answer. Widderman rounded the desk, came out of the office with him, and pressed the button for the lift. It came up, and Widderman opened the door. The little attendant wasn't there.

"I don't think there's room for the two of us, so will you see yourself down?" asked Widderman. "And thank you for your frankness."

"It might prove a good morning's work," Roger said. He put out his hand. Widderman hesitated, as if in surprise, then took it; his clasp was firm, his hand cool. "I'll be in touch," Roger promised, and stepped into the lift, pressing the *Ground Floor* button. Widderman closed the door.

Roger stood frowning as the lift began to go down, knowing that Widderman might have fooled him very cleverly, yet more than half persuaded that he knew more of the truth about the man. Muriel Kennedy seemed much more bitter than Widderman himself.

The lift jerked. Roger looked at the trellis work gate of another floor, as the lift jerked and jolted again, as if it were coming to a standstill. He felt a momentary alarm, but that subsided as the movement became smoother; he must be nearly at the ground floor by now.

The lift jerked again, quivered violently, and then dropped like a stone.

14

JOLT

FEAR flared up in Roger in that split second. He was helplessly trapped, and there was nothing at all he could do but stab the *Emergency* button. Nothing happened when he did, and next moment the lift crashed.

He felt agonising jarring at his knees, was flung against one side, banging his head on a wooden peg, then flung to the other, crashing against the iron trellis of the gate. But he was still standing. There was pain in his legs, but not the numbness of a break. He heard someone shout.

It was hard to realise that there was no further danger, that the lift was at the bottom of its shaft, and there was nothing more to worry about. His head was aching from the savage jolt. He moved his right leg, and found it uninjured; tested his left, and was able to stand on it. Apart from the shaking up, he was all right.

Footsteps rang out on stone steps, and then the small youth who had taken him up to Widderman's office appeared, face gargoyle-like in alarm.

He squeaked: "*Are you all right?*"

"I'm all right," muttered Roger. He felt as if someone had cracked him on the back of the head, then swiped him behind the knees. "Get me out of here."

"J-j-just a minute," the lad stammered. He pulled at the outer gate; it jammed, and for a moment Roger felt a flash of angry impatience. Then the door slid open, and Roger opened the inner door.

"The—the—the cable broke!" the lad gasped. He was very small, very pale, and had big eyes like glass marbles. "I couldn't believe it when I saw it going past, I just—" He broke off, gasping.

"All right, let's take it easy," Roger said, and leaned against a table for support. "Are you sure the cable snapped?"

"I saw the ends as it passed the ground floor," the lad said. "It—it—it looks as if it's been cut. Two men came in to service it, though, only half an hour ago. I can't understand—"

*   *   *   *   *

The preliminary report from the elevator mechanics and the Yard engineers who examined the lift at Widderman's premises confirmed that the cable had been cut with wire-cutters. It made another thing obvious, too. The safety mechanism had been tampered with—a simple matter of disconnecting an electric wire. Someone had made quite sure that the lift would crash. The experts were agreed on one thing: someone who knew the principle on which the lift worked must have caused the damage, and anyone with the right equipment could have done it quickly. Two men posing as service mechanics had come while Roger had been with Widderman, but the little youth had never seen them before, and hope of tracing them seemed remote.

"Sure it was while I was with Widderman?" Roger asked.

"Yes, sir," answered a detective sergeant who had come back from inspecting the damaged lift. He was a thin, rather dyspeptic-looking individual, with a whining note in his voice. "It's not used much except by Mr. Widderman and his secretary. It was installed four years ago when Widderman broke his leg, and couldn't get up and down the stairs."

"And it could have been meant for him?"

"For him, for the secretary, or for you," declared the sergeant.

"Yes, of course," said Roger. "Thanks."

He waited until the man went out, considered the situation for several minutes, but saw nothing new in the report which had just been made. Slowly he lifted the telephone and asked Hardy if he could spare him ten minutes.

"You stay where you are," Hardy ordered. "I'm told you ought to keep off your legs as much as you can for a day or two. I'll be along in five minutes."

Roger replaced the receiver, looked across at Cope, and cocked his thumb towards the door; complainingly, Cope got up.

"I know, I know," he grumbled. "Let me ask you this, Handsome. How much of Widderman's cock-and-bull story do you believe?"

"Everything or nothing," Roger answered.

Cope went out, grimacing. Roger shifted his position gingerly, for there was increasing pain in his right knee. An X-ray photograph had revealed that nothing was broken, but the knee was heavily bandaged. Roger would get a lot of discomfort, and his movements would be restricted for the next two or three days.

He read a report which had come in from one of the men watching Rocky Marlo. Rocky had posted a parcel late the previous night to someone c/o the Post Office, Piccadilly. The Yard man trailing Rocky had not been able to read the name on the parcel, because that had been written, and the address itself printed, in block capitals. There were indications that Marlo was agitated, though, and there was a report on the incident when the men who had visited Horace Green had come away with their heads shaved. The report added:

> *Although both men usually go about bare-headed, both are now wearing cloth caps pulled low over their heads.*

Cope had pencilled a note:

> *Don't look as if they got much change out of Green. No news of Green.*

The door opened, and Hardy came in.

"All right, don't try to get up," he said, and came quickly across to the chair on the other side of Roger's desk. "I've just had a word with Dr. McKenzie. He says you ought to take at least two days off, and keep your legs up."

"He's crazy."

"I daresay," said Hardy. "But that's what you're going to do. You could have trouble for weeks if you use those legs too much now. Think the job was meant for you?"

"It's possible, but hardly likely, surely," Roger said. "No one knew where I was going, and I wasn't in the place for an hour. If it was meant for me, it was pretty quick work. But there's a lot to indicate that someone is after Widderman."

"Tell me about it," Hardy ordered.

He listened intently for the next twenty minutes, without making any written notes, and he was quiet for several minutes afterwards. Then he commented:

"No one would be killed in that lift, would they?"

"Not unless it crashed from top to bottom. Even then the most likely thing would be a broken leg, and severe bruising."

"Murder not intended," Hardy remarked. He pursed his lips. "And you think Widderman's on the side of the angels, according to his lights?"

"It's how I saw the situation."

"Hm, yes. This secretary—Muriel Kennedy."

"Yes."

"Jim Kennedy's daughter?"

"Yes."

"I knew her up to the age of thirteen or fourteen," said Hardy, as if with an effort. "She must be thirty-five or so now. Her only sister died in a car crash a year or two before the corruption trouble, and Muriel played a lot with my boy, Peter." Hardy didn't remind Roger that his son had died from polio, fifteen years ago. "Funny thing, we used to think that Peter and Muriel might make a match of it. Funny what parents will think, isn't it? And she's still bitter?"

"Very."

"Say anything about her father?"

"No—and Widderman has kept it pretty quiet that he had Kennedy as a consultant. We don't know how long that's been going on."

"No," said Hardy. "Sensible thing to do, though, if you want to sail as close to the wind as you can. Only a policeman can hope to guess what the police will take seriously, and what they'll wink at. Hm. Marlo your chief suspect?"

Roger said: "It looks as if Marlo's running round in circles, he's so scared—and that isn't like him. He seems to have run into some kind of trouble with Green, the brush salesman, too. It looks to me as if someone might be trying to put a finger on both Marlo and Widderman."

Hardy said: "Who?"

"I'd like to know, too," Roger said drily. "I know what I'll do while I'm laid up."

Hardy smiled. "That's more sensible! What?"

"I'll get my wife to put a bed-chair in the sitting-room so that I can put my legs up," Roger said. "And I'll have the police witnesses we're worried about come and see me. Birwitz can go and get them, and we needn't handle this angle from the Yard at all."

"Good idea," approved Hardy, unhesitatingly.

Ten minutes after Hardy had gone, Cope came in, obviously excited.

"Just had a report from Radlett," he said. "The new owner of *Zipp* is dear old pal Kennedy. How about that? He's always had an interest, through an associated company, and a couple of months ago, he took over. I thought you'd like to know."

* * * * *

Birwitz reported at the Bell Street house in the middle of that afternoon.

Roger, wearing grey flannels and an old sports jacket, and sitting with his legs up on a bed-chair, told him exactly what he required. By five o'clock, the detective officer who had made a hash of giving his evidence against Widderman was sitting opposite Roger; Birwitz was standing by the fireplace, where a coal fire burned red and warm.

The D.O., a man named Cotten, was in his middle-thirties. Roger knew him as sound rather than brilliant. There were lines at the corners of his eyes, which seemed to be of strain and anxiety. Although he looked physically fit, there was a hint of edginess about the way he clenched his hands, and the way he sat stiffly on an upright chair. Edginess wasn't surprising in the circumstances; the question was whether there was any deeper reason for it.

"... I'm telling you what I told Mr. Cope, sir," Cotten declared. "I got confused in the box. That solicitor tied me up, until I didn't know whether I was coming or going. I know it was asking for trouble, and I know it's a pretty poor show for a detective officer, but that's the truth of it."

"No one bribed you?"

"No, sir."

"Can your bank account, or your wife's expense account, stand up to examination?"

"I don't mind what inquiries you make, sir. We rub along on my salary, that's about all. Promotion to the C.I.D. was just what we needed. It meant another three quid a week, but—well, we managed before and I suppose we'll manage again."

"You mean, if you're sent back to uniform?"

Cotten began: "Yes, sir," and then caught his breath. Something like dread appeared in his pale brown eyes. "Mr. West, it won't be worse than that, will it? I haven't done anything wrong, I—"

"If this was just a question of being tied up in knots by a smart lawyer, you won't even go back to uniform," Roger said. "Any serious money worries?"

"No, sir. We've always got by, as I told you."

"Any family worries?"

Cotten hesitated, and then said: "Well—"

Roger asked quickly: "Any children, Cotten?"

"Yes, sir, two boys and a girl."

"How old?"

"The boys are still at school."

"The girl?"

"She's—she's nineteen, sir."

"What does she do for a living?"

Cotten didn't answer, and all his colour faded. Birwitz caught the implication of this reaction as quickly as Roger did; that was obvious from the way he stared at Cotten, and the way he raised his hand, as if to draw attention to what this might mean. Roger sensed the mood of excitement in Birwitz, as well as the unhappiness in Cotten. He did not waste time.

"Worried about your daughter, Cotten?"

"I—I am a bit, sir."

"Why?"

"Well, she—well, she's always been a bit flighty. You know what young people are like these days. She —well, she got mixed up with a Teddy Boy mob, in Soho. She—as a matter of fact, sir, she left home about three months ago, and we haven't heard from her. It's nearly killed my wife, Mr. West, the worry of it." Now the man's voice was pitched very low, and he had difficulty in controlling it.

"How bad is the situation?" asked Roger, quietly.

Cotten closed his eyes. It was a long time before he opened them, and answered.

"If my wife knew the truth, sir, I think it would kill her. I really do. My Jane's gone—gone just about as bad as a girl can. She's a dance hostess at a Soho club, and there isn't any doubt about it, she's ready to sleep with anyone for a few pounds. It's an awful thing to say about your own daughter, but—"

"All right, Cotten," Roger interrupted, gently. "If you've had that on your mind it isn't surprising you got muddled with your evidence. Does Jane work at one of Widderman's clubs?"

"I don't know for sure, sir. I know it's a place where Rocky Marlo's men get together. There was a row between Widderman and Marlo a couple of years ago, but I was never sure it was genuine—looked to me as if it might be a phoney break-up, so that one could play off against the other. But it doesn't make much difference where Jane's concerned. She—she took this on because the life appealed to her. And I hoped that I might be able to help her a bit, as I was at the Yard and usually in the Soho district. I don't mind admitting it's been hell," Cotten went on, and now he began to dab at his damp forehead. "Absolute hell, sir. What with the boys asking where she's gone, and my wife almost off her head with worry, and—and me knowing that I ought to ask for a transfer to one of the Divisions, but wanting to be around Soho in case Jane needed help. It's been plain bloody hell, that's the truth of it—and I knew it would run me into trouble, sooner or later. As a matter of fact—"

He broke off, but Roger did not prompt him. When he went on, it was in a low-pitched voice, and he was dabbing his forehead more vigorously all the time.

"As a matter of fact, Mr. West, I hated the whole Soho set-up so much that I began to wonder just what I *was* saying on oath. Did I want to get Widderman behind bars because he was part of the set-up, or— Well, you can see what I mean, sir."

"Yes, I know exactly what you mean," Roger said.

*   *   *   *   *

Far from having been corrupted by money, Cotten had made a torment for himself by trying to be completely objective. He was exactly what the Yard had always believed, a sound and conscientious officer, less ambitious and less promising than Birwitz, but a policeman through and through.

When he had gone, Birwitz said: "I wonder how many more of us are in a mess, sir?"

"Meaning?"

Birwitz said: "Well, someone strung me along until I was a bag of nerves. Cotten's a bag of nerves, too."

Roger said: "Yes. If we believe the indications, at least seven officers have made a hash of giving evidence so that a police case failed. Each man may be living on his nerves. Is that just coincidence?" When Birwitz made no comment, Roger went on: "If there was any connection between the people who were found not guilty, it would make sense. There isn't, as far as we know yet."

"If there is one, I'll find it," Birwitz said grimly. "Going to see anyone else tonight?"

"Go and get Ayreton, from Lambeth, will you?" Roger asked.

"Right."

"And, Birwitz."

"Yes, sir?"

"No approach to your wife or you yet?"

"Nothing at all," Birwitz assured him.

Roger nodded, and the sergeant went out.

Roger was sitting back, glooming about the possibility that Birwitz would not be approached, when Janet came in with some tea, and a letter which had come by the second post. On the instant, Roger recognised the kind of buff-coloured envelope which would be so familiar to Birwitz. He frowned at it, glanced at Janet as she poured out tea, and pretended not to be interested. As soon as she had left him alone, he opened the letter.

Were they starting on him?

The letter read:

*DON'T TELL ME YOU TRUST HARDY.
HE'S AS CORRUPT AS THEY CAN BE,
ALWAYS TAKING HAND-OUTS. HE MUST
BE WORTH A FORTUNE.*

Roger's first reaction was of relief that this wasn't an attempt to poison his mind against Janet, but the second came quickly: This is scurrilous nonsense, he thought.

Then, unbidden, a question sprang into his mind. *Was* it nonsense? Was Hardy incorruptible?

"I'm losing my grip," Roger said aloud.

But he failed to still his disquiet.

15

WEAK SPOTS

AYRETON was thirty-one, fair-haired, spindly, with very full lips and pale blue eyes. There was relief in those eyes now, as if a great weight had been lifted from his shoulders. In Roger's hand were three letters, each typewritten; Birwitz held a fourth.

"It was driving me round the bend," Ayreton declared. He had a faint Irish brogue, and spoke rather in a sing-song. "It was the only skeleton in my cupboard, Mr. West, and it had been there such a long time I'd almost forgotten it. Then I had the first of these letters."

Roger looked down, to read again:

WHAT DO YOU THINK YOUR CHIEF WOULD THINK OF YOU IF HE KNEW YOU TOOK BRIBES?

"At first I hardly remembered what it was about," said Ayreton. "And I wouldn't have taken the money but for the sergeant on duty with me. He's been out of the Force for six years, and—" Ayreton broke off, moistened his lips, and went on: "Don't misunderstand me, sir. I don't take any pride in it. I took the drop for blinking at parking offences, and the fact that my sergeant did the same makes no difference. As a matter of fact, sir, he was retired early for similar offences, and he could have given me away if he'd wanted to. He chose not to, so—"

Roger interrupted: "Could he have sent you these letters?"

"I don't see why he should," Ayreton answered. "He's living in a little bungalow in Devon, and I believe he raises a few chickens. It would be more likely to come from the men who—who gave us the hand-out."

"Do you remember them?"

"Yes, sir."

"Can you name them?"

Ayreton said: "One was Saul Widderman, sir."

"How many were there?"

"Three," said Ayreton. "There was Widderman, and there was Jim Kennedy—I knew he'd been fired from the Force, but that happened before my time."

"Who was the third man?" asked Roger.

"I don't remember his name," said Ayreton. "He was the boss of a firm which manufactured brushes—household brushes and that kind of thing. He had a team of house-to-house salesmen, and a lot of them had cars. They used to double park for odd half-hours, and the Boss dropped me a pound a week to blink at it. All this happened eight years ago, sir. I was pretty fresh to the beat at that time. I used to tell myself that there wasn't any harm in it, but—" He broke off, shrugging his shoulders. "I've paid for it this past year."

"Since these letters started coming?"

"Yes, sir."

"Have you been asked to give false evidence, or look the other way?"

"No, sir. But I don't mind admitting I've felt that I was being watched wherever I went, and when I reported to the Yard for duty on the day I first got these letters, I felt like death. My God, I've regretted what I did!" Ayreton brushed his hand across his forehead, and went on gruffly: "What disciplinary action will be taken, sir? I'd rather know, so that I can warn my wife that there might be—well, trouble."

Roger said: "It's not up to me, Ayreton, but as it's so long ago you'll probably get no more than a sharp reprimand. You might be put back in uniform for a while, but—" he shrugged. "My job is to find out why you boobed on this evidence, and to make sure you aren't taking the drop now."

"I swear I've told you the whole truth, sir."

"Right," said Roger. "Go back home, report for duty in the usual way tomorrow, and take it easy. Thanks for coming across with the whole story."

"It's a big relief to have talked, sir."

"Sure you've no idea who sent the letters?"

"No idea at all," Ayreton assured him.

When he had gone, Birwitz rubbed the palms of his hands together, and said:

"So either Kennedy or Widderman could have known that Ayreton was wide open to pressure."

"So would anyone they've told," Roger pointed out.

He pinned one of the letters on to a sheet of cardboard, alongside the letter which Birwitz had shown him. With Birwitz bending over his shoulder, he compared the paper and the typewriting. There was no shadow of doubt; this was the same kind of paper, and the same machine had been used. There were slight deformities in the letter 'k', and the 'u' and certain other letters were out of alignment.

"An Olivetti portable, pica type," Birwitz said. "There are tens of thousands of them."

"Yes. Our first job is to find out who owns one among our list of half suspects. And we want to find out if anyone else has received these letters. We'll call it a day," Roger added. "But have Simmons, from Whitechapel, over here by nine o'clock in the morning, will you?"

"On the dot," growled Birwitz.

"Any kind of approach from the other side yet?"

"No," said Birwitz. "I'm beginning to doubt whether that's coming off."

He sounded as if he was sorry.

*   *   *   *   *

Two more of the men who had gone back on their statements when giving evidence proved to have been under considerable emotional strain.

A man in the East End was in almost identical plight with Birwitz, but there was one big difference: his wife had a boy-friend. This man had received letters typed on the same machine and the same paper.

Another, at Highgate, received letters telling him that his only son was a thief, and that at any moment he would be found out. The boy had denied it, the mother had defended him; the detective had been walking a tightrope of family dissension for over a year.

"And we know about these," Hardy said to Roger, on the morning of the second day after the lift crash. "There could be dozens of others."

Roger said: "The problem is going to be to dig them out."

He was testing his knee in front of the window, feeling a twinge or two of pain, but sure that he could go to the Yard for normal duty. He could not see any way of finding out if others were being affected in the same way, except by putting out a general request to the Divisions for the names of any men who showed signs of overwork or other tensions.

He went to the Yard later, and was sitting at his desk in the middle of the afternoon, with all the reports spread out in front of him, and his mind buzzing with facts, when that idea occurred to him. He called Hardy.

"Come in at once," Hardy said, and when Roger went into his office, he asked: "What have you got?"

"We could ask Divisions for the names of anyone who is showing signs of overwork or strain," said Roger eagerly. "Put out a memo saying that we're worried about it, because of the shortage of men, and that we don't want anyone to go on for too long without a break—that kind of thing. If you make it an official memo, I'll start tackling the men individually. It won't look so odd."

"It might work," Hardy said. "We'll try it."

*   *   *   *   *

A week later, Roger and Birwitz had interviewed another thirty-two men. All but five admitted that they were suffering from more than overwork; fourteen had been receiving poison pen or blackmailing letters, and family anxieties affected the others.

*   *   *   *   *

"It's as if someone's trying to start a rot in the whole police force," Hardy said, "and is working on the weakest spots."

"That's about it," Roger replied grimly. He wondered what his chief would say if he knew about the letter naming him. No more had come, but the shadowed doubts about Hardy's incorruptibility were still there. Roger had deliberately not reported it; it could fog the issue, making it impossible for Hardy to be objective. Hardy had given him *carte blanche*, so he was taking advantage of that.

"Do you seriously think that starting a rot is possible?" Hardy demanded.

"It's possible because it's actually happening," Roger answered. "Every divisional station, every sub station, every department here at the Yard, has one or two men on its strength affected by some secret anxiety—an anxiety they haven't been able to report to their senior officers. Once they began to keep it to themselves, it became like a festering sore. And we haven't even begun to check the uniformed branch. On the credit side is an unspecified Olivetti typewriter, and some rumours. We've got to find that typewriter. I'm going to start on Rocky Marlo, and find an excuse to raid his place. Is that all right?"

"Just make sure you've got your search warrant."

"I'll get a search warrant," Roger said gruffly. "And then I'm going to search all of Widderman's clubs and offices. He gave me permission verbally. If he doesn't confirm it, I'll find an excuse for a search."

"Make sure the excuse will stand up," Hardy advised. "The papers didn't moan much about Birwitz coming back to work, but we don't want to take any risk of setting them off on it again."

Roger didn't speak, and after a moment's hesitation, Hardy went on: "Have you any idea what is behind it?"

"No."

"Try a guess."

"I can't," said Roger, exasperatedly. "There's nothing to base an intelligent guess on. We've lost a

number of prosecutions, either because of astute lawyers
or because of ineptitude on the part of some of our
chaps. There's no evidence at all to suggest that the
lawyers have done more than take advantage of witnesses who were obviously unsure of themselves. Apart
from that, there's only the evidence that someone is
working like crazy to weaken the structure of the C.I.D.
The first place to start is in the lower ranks—and it's
started in a big way. Now there's a real danger of it
spreading high and wide. It could be because someone's got some big coup in mind, a coup which will
stand a better chance of succeeding if the Force is
standing on one leg. It could even be that someone just
hates the guts of the police. It—" he broke off.

Hardy said: "Or of the Assistant Commissioner for
the Criminal Investigation Department."

"What are you saying?" Roger demanded sharply.

Hardy said: "I told you before, Handsome, that I
had more to do with Kennedy's dismissal from the
Force than any man. I was also responsible for clearing
out a dozen other officers under charges of corruption.
Now, if one of them is getting back at me—"

"Do you mean Kennedy?"

"I'm just asking you to keep that in mind as a motive,"
Hardy said, with almost painful deliberation. He stood
up, and began to walk about the office. Obviously there
was something in his mind, something more than Roger
yet knew, something he hated to talk about. Suddenly,
he stopped in front of Roger, and put his right hand
to his inside coat pocket. Roger, still sitting down, kept
very still.

Slowly, Hardy took out a buff-coloured envelope. He
held it for a moment, then handed it to Roger. It was
addressed to him at the Yard, and marked: *Private &
Confidential*. It was typewritten, and the capital P was
slightly out of alignment, like that on the machine
used for the other letters. "Open it," Hardy said.

Roger slid a finger into the envelope and took out the

sheet of paper inside—paper of a dirty-looking colour and poor quality, exactly like the paper on the letter which Birwitz had received; which the others had received; which he, Roger, had received.

It said:

YOU'VE GOT A LOT TO BE PROUD OF, YOU HAVE. THE YARD'S SPLIT RIGHT OPEN WITH GRAFT AND CORRUPTION AND IT WILL GET WORSE. THE BEST THING FOR YOU IS TO GET OUT WHILE THE GOING'S GOOD.

Roger read it, quickly at first, then very slowly; and he was keenly aware of Hardy's steady gaze. It was difficult to decide what to say, but he said at last:

"Is this the first one?"

"Yes."

"When did it come?"

"This morning."

"Any telephone calls or threats, or—?"

"Just that, out of the blue."

Roger said: "It's really hotting up." At least he would not have to tell Hardy about the letter he had had. He pushed his chair back, and stood up, completely forgetting his injured knees, and they did not give him a twinge. "I've been trying to think what he might try next. I hadn't thought of this, but—there's one obvious thing."

"What?"

"A newspaper campaign against the Yard. Anything which could stir up mud."

"Yes," Hardy said. "That's what I'm afraid of. That's why I've shown you this before I've shown it to anyone else. The Commissioner will have to see it today, of course, but I haven't any doubt that he'll confirm what I've told you. Get to the bottom of it, Handsome."

Roger said, "You bet your life I will."

He left Hardy's office a few minutes later, feeling as if he had been caught in a storm. It was still hard to believe how deep this went, hard to believe how deadly it could become. He went along to his office. There would be no difficulty in arranging the search warrants; the only question was how quickly he should get them. He reached the decision to act at once.

Cope was at the telephone; he broke off as Roger entered, and said:

"It's Birwitz. Will you talk to him?"

"Yes," said Roger, and took the telephone and said: "West speaking."

"Mr. West, it's—" Birwitz began, and it was immediately obvious that he was feeling excited. Roger's heart began to pound. "It's started just as you said it would," Birwitz burst out. "I've been offered fifty quid for some inside information. Do I go ahead?"

The break had come, Roger thought, and immediately felt something of Birwitz's excitement. This could be the beginning of the end. He had guessed right about how the other side would operate, and when guesses went right luck often stayed in.

"You certainly go ahead," he said.

When Birwitz rang off, Roger glanced across at Cope, who was writing, and wondered what Cope would say if he knew what had been planned. Gradually, excitement dulled. He began to wonder uneasily if he was doing the right thing. Until the case was over he would be subject to these moods of doubt.

Then the telephone rang, bringing relief from self-questioning, and the operator said:

"The newspaperman, Mr. Anvill, would like to talk to you, sir. He says it's personal and urgent."

16

HOTTING UP

"HALLO, Anvill," Roger asked. "What can I do for you?"

"It's what I can do for you," Anvill said. "I don't want to talk about it on the telephone. Can you meet me in about half an hour's time?"

"I should think so," Roger said, trying not to appear over-anxious. "Where will you be?"

"Do you know the Old Fox, in Chane Court, Fleet Street?"

"Yes, but it'll take me half an hour to get there at this time of day," Roger said. "Make it an hour's time, will you—just before twelve."

"I'll buy you the famous Old Fox steak pudding," Anvill promised, and added after a pause: "How are things going?"

"Pretty well."

"Is that official optimism, or do you mean it?" demanded Anvill. He didn't wait for an answer, just gave a short laugh, and rang off. Roger put the receiver down thoughtfully.

Cope was scribbling some notes, as if anxious that he should not forget anything, and he didn't look up. Roger rang the Sergeants' Room, and arranged for a driver to take him to Fleet Street; he still avoided driving himself, for in emergency his knees might let him down. He did not brood over Anvill's call; he would soon know all about that, and had plenty of other things to worry about.

He called Widderman.

"I'm sorry, but Mr. Widderman is in conference with his club managers," Muriel Kennedy said, the frostiness still in her voice.

"Ask him to speak to me, will you?" Roger said mildly. "It's very urgent." He wondered if she would make difficulties, but she did not; and a moment later he heard her talking to Widderman, before the man came on the line.

"Yes, Mr. West?"

"Do you recall giving me permission to search your clubs and offices?"

"I do."

"I'd like to arrange it this afternoon."

After a moment's pause, Widderman said: "Very well. I will instruct Miss Kennedy, and she will make the necessary arrangements." He did not ask what the search was about, and rang off without another word. Roger put the receiver down, sharply this time. Cope finished his notes, and looked up:

"He going to play?"

"Yes. Lay all the searches on, will you? We're looking for anything that might help us, and especially the Olivetti typewriter on which this was written." Roger gave Cope one of the letters which had no-one's name on it, quite sure that Cope would get this laid on quickly and efficiently; and he told Birwitz what was being planned.

*   *   *   *   *

About that time, the telephone bell rang in the Birwitz's house, and Meg hurried from the kitchen to answer it. A man whose voice she did not recognise asked for Witzy.

"He's not at home," Meg said. "I don't know when to expect him, I'm afraid."

"That's too bad, Mrs. B.," the man said jeeringly. "You just tell Birwitz to call Whitechapel 9851, see. And tell him to be quick about it, or he'll really be in trouble. Whitechapel 9851. Got that?"

"I've got it," Meg said. She rang off, put the receiver down slowly, and stood and stared at the wall for a few seconds, hating all that was happening, frightened because there were factors which she knew nothing about. She made herself lift the telephone again, put in a call to the Yard, and asked for Witzy. When he came through, she said:

"I've had another message, Witzy—he wants you to call this number." She hesitated, and then read the number out. "Whitechapel 9851."

"Okay, sweetie," Birwitz said. "You needn't worry."

That was like pretending she was a child; of course she would worry, the danger had never been greater.

*   *   *   *   *

"Tell him anything he wants to know, and tell him that we might raid *Zipp* Brushes," Roger ordered. "Let me know what's happened at once. Go out and make the call from a call-box."

"Right, sir," said Birwitz.

He used a call-box five minutes' walk away from Scotland Yard, and after dialling the number, he stared at the traffic going towards Westminster Bridge, and the masses of people walking, and began to think that any of them might be involved in this affair. He heard the ringing sound going on and on, and it continued for so long that he half-wondered whether the message was a hoax.

Then a man answered, in a Cockney voice:

"Who's that?"

"Birwitz," Birwitz said, and his heart missed a beat.

"Okay, okay, you're a wide one," the man said, and a note of satisfaction was clear in his voice. "Listen, Birwitz, I want some information, and you know what will happen if I don't get it."

Birwitz said: "I know."

"And you'd better remember," the other said, softly.

"Okay—just tell me what I want to know. I've heard a rumour that there are going to be police raids on Soho this afternoon—on some of the clubs. Is that right?"

"Yes."

"Any other raids planned?" demanded the man, and there was a catch in his voice. "Come on, tell me, any other raids planned?"

"They might have a go at *Zipp*," Birwitz answered.

"So they *might*," breathed the other man. "Call this number, if they are. Got that? Call this number."

*   *   *   *   *

At ten minutes to twelve, Roger got out of the police car in Fleet Street, and told the driver to be back at half past one; that was as long as he wanted to spend with Anvill over luncheon.

Fleet Street was in its usual bustle, and there was an almost stationary line of cars, trucks, newspaper vans and buses from Chancery Lane to Ludgate Circus. Roger glanced along Fleet Street, saw the great dome of St. Paul's still in full, dominating sight, and wondered vaguely if the planners would eventually put up a high building that would hide it from here. Then he walked along the narrow passage to Chane Court, which was not far from the little Court where the Cheshire Cheese had been for centuries. The Old Fox was a smaller pub, equally famous for its old English steak pies and puddings, a tiny remnant of Elizabethan London still boasting its original oak beams and its twisting staircase, its enormous cellars, even the manhole which dropped down to the old Fleet River, now only a tiny trickle of water.

The cobbles underfoot made walking treacherous, and Roger took more care than usual, acutely conscious of his bandaged knee, wondering how long it would be before he could forget that sharp, frightening fall in the lift. There was still no evidence against the perpetrator; no certainty that the cable had been cut for his benefit, or for Widderman's.

He passed a narrow alley, also cobbled, which led

along the side of the Old Fox. Over the front door of the pub a sign-post, painted gilt on black, and in old English lettering, outlined the history of both the pub and Chane Court; and a plaque on the wall announced:

Samuel Pepys
Samuel Johnson
Charles Dickens
Were all regular visitors
to this hostelry

He turned to go into the pub, up three wooden steps, when a man called quietly:

"Mr. West."

Roger turned round, half expecting to see his sergeant. Instead, he saw a stranger, a pleasant-looking, clean-cut young man, in the entrance to the passage alongside the Old Fox.

"Yes?" Roger said.

"Are you expecting Mr. Anvill?"

"That's right."

"He's found something along here which he thinks will interest you," the young man said. "Can you spare a minute?"

Roger turned again, gingerly. "Yes, of course." He went forward, puzzled, but not in the slightest degree suspicious; it did not enter his head that he might be walking into a trap, that another attack could come as swiftly as that at the lift.

The young man stood aside. Roger went into the alley, picking his way cautiously over cobbles which were even more uneven here. Twenty yards along was a turning, which led behind the Old Fox, probably to the yard where it kept its stores and took deliveries.

"Just round to the left, sir."

Roger turned left. There was the yard, with some out-houses, crooked with lichen—the clock turned back by hundreds of years. He saw no one. That was the moment when he first began to wonder whether he had walked into a trap, and swung round. The sudden movement was too sharp, and a twinge of pain shot through his left knee—and on the instant fear flamed up in him. The pleasant-looking young man was just in front of him, right arm raised, a long iron bar in it. His face was very pale, his lips set tightly, and he brought the weapon down with a sweeping blow as if he meant to kill.

Roger's left knee gave way.

He lost his balance, fell, and felt the end of the weapon catch his right shoulder, but without any great force. As it did so, he realised that out of his weakness came his one chance to save himself. He shot out his right hand, grasped the man's ankle, tugged and felt the man stagger. Then heard him gasp. He himself felt a sudden, almost paralysing blow on the back of the head, and cried out with pain; but he did not lose consciousness, and he saw the man reeling backwards, saw him fall heavily and awkwardly. The iron bar caught Roger on the forehead, then clattered on the cobbles. Through tears of pain, he saw it just in front of him, quivering. He sat still for at least a minute, while the wound pounded in his head, until gradually the pain lifted. His assailant was trying to scramble up. Roger poked the iron bar between his legs and sent him crashing again.

There was a wild look in the man's eyes.

Roger called: "*Police!*" in a voice as loud as he could, and heard footsteps at the end of the alley. "*Police!*" he shouted, and got to his knees. Two young girls, skirts so short that they looked like ballet dancers, reached the end of the alley, and stood staring, each holding the other's hand. "Fetch the police!" Roger called. A youth appeared in black jacket and striped trousers, with a bowler square on his head.

"He—he wants the police," one of the girls said nervously.

The man who had attacked Roger was trying to get up again. Roger said roughly:

"Move any more, and I'll crack your skull." He used the piece of iron as a walking stick, and heaved himself on to his feet, then saw the girls run off, and the youth come forward cautiously.

"Are you—are you all right?"

"Have those girls gone for the police?"

"Yes."

"Thanks," Roger said. "I'm from Scotland Yard."

He stood over his assailant, the pain no longer so bad, but feeling a curious warmth on the back of his head, where the iron bar had caught him; and he saw the young man staring at his forehead. He felt giddy, swayed, and let himself rest against the wall, for support. Something red appeared in front of his eyes. Then the youth cried: "*Look out!*" The man on the floor snatched his right hand from his pocket, and Roger saw the glint of steel. He lunged forward, smacking the iron bar against the blade, and the blow twisted the knife round in the man's hand; suddenly blood welled up from a cut across the palm. The young man exclaimed: "*God!*" Then footsteps sounded loudly from the passage, and two uniformed policemen came running, with the girls behind them and a stream of people in their wake.

One man exclaimed: "Mr. *West.*"

"Yes," Roger said, heavily. "Get this chap to Bow Street, on a charge of assault. Look after his hand."

"Your head, sir!"

"Head?"

"It's bleeding."

"Nothing to worry about," said Roger, impatiently. But now he understood the red mist in front of his right eye, and when he brushed his hand over his forehead it came away wet with blood.

He was glad when the uniformed men took over, and men from the crowd helped. He was guided into the men's lavatory at the Old Fox, a man washed his head then examined it closely; Roger saw a wound, little more than a two inch cut, on his forehead, certainly nothing to worry about, although it was bleeding so freely.

"If we can stop the bleeding it will be all right," said the man who had brought him in here. "The best thing would be to go to a doctor. There's one in my building. He—"

"Later, thanks," Roger said gruffly. "I'll use a towel as a pad." He folded a small linen hand towel, pressed it against the wound, and went on: "I'll be all right. Will you find out if a Mr. Anvill is waiting in the pub?"

"Anvill of the *Globe*?"

"Yes."

"Haven't seen him," the man said, wryly. "I'm from the *Echo*, and if Anvill was here I would know. Expecting him?"

"Yes."

"Dark doings, when the Yard and a *Globe* man have an appointment," said the other, with a grin. "I'll go through and check, though. Are you sure you'll be all right here?"

"Quite sure," said Roger.

The little cloakroom had a window which overlooked the yard of the Old Fox, and he was glad to open it wide, so that the clear fresh air could float in. The cobbled yard was piled high with crates and barrels, some full, some empty, water coming from a waste pipe and splashing on to one of the barrels. No one was out there now, but the men who had taken away his assailant would soon be back.

Meanwhile he had a new problem: about Anvill.

It was inconceivable that Anvill or any prominent newspaperman would lend himself to an attack of this kind, but it was just possible that the speaker on the telephone had imitated the *Globe* man's voice. Roger leaned against the handbasin, finding relaxation in his cigarette, looking out of the window, wondering whether the head wound was as slight as he wanted to make out.

Then he saw the brim of a hat behind one of the barrels. He first noticed it because water was splashing nearby and making a little pool, so that he stared at it more intently, and recognised it for what it was. Why should a hat be out there? It looked in good condition, a curly brimmed trilby if he was any judge. He frowned. Then someone came along to the cloakroom, and Roger went out, his heart beginning to beat with greater agitation.

He opened the door leading to the courtyard, and heard footsteps coming along the alley-way; these were his policemen. He limped past a pile of crates towards the hat, then round a wooden barrel which stood waist-high.

There was Anvill, and Anvill's hat lay a few inches from his right shoulder. There was an ugly wound in his head, which had bled freely and was still bleeding. He lay on his back, as if he had been dragged over the cobbles and flung there out of sight.

Roger moistened his lips as he went forward. Bending down wasn't comfortable, for the blood rushed to his head, but he had to find out how Anvill was. The man looked more dead than alive; seen from this angle he certainly did not appear to be breathing.

Roger squeezed between the wall and the barrel, and felt for the man's wrist. For a moment he detected nothing, and he feared that Anvill was dead; but when he shifted his forefinger he felt the faint beating of the pulse. He stood up and raised his voice, and the policemen came hurrying.

*   *   *   *   *

It was half an hour before Anvill was taken off in an ambulance; half an hour in which the crowds gathered at the entrances to Chane Court, while plainclothes-men from Division arrived for the necessary routine, and while a first-aid man who had come with the ambulance snipped hair away from the cut on Roger's head, and then put on a dressing and some plaster.

"It won't be comfortable, but it shouldn't take long to heal, sir," he said.

"Thanks," said Roger. He looked up, to see Birwitz forcing his way through the crowd, and had seldom been more pleased to see a man. "Birwitz," he said, "I want you to go over to the *Globe* offices and see if you can find out why Anvill wanted me, and what it was all about."

"Right, sir," Birwitz said. "You're going home, aren't you?"

"I'm going to see this chap who tried to crack my skull," said Roger.

17

COINCIDENCE?

THE man who had attacked Roger behind the Old Fox was sitting in the cell, under charge. His right hand was heavily bandaged, and there was dried blood from the wound on his trousers and on his coat. There was a bruise on one side of his chin, too, and he had a slightly discoloured eye. In spite of his injuries, there was something aggressive about him; he looked as if he might try to break out of his prison at any moment.

The Divisional Detective Inspector who had examined him with Roger was a tall, fair-haired man named McClean who looked as Scottish as he sounded.

"I've told him it will be good for him if he talks, but he will not say a word," McClean said.

"What did you find in his pockets?" asked Roger.

"Not a great deal," McClean answered, "but enough to identify him, no doubt. He's a door-to-door brush salesman, named—"

"*What?*" exclaimed Roger.

"Och, he looks as if he does pretty well out of selling a few brushes," said McClean. "Who can tell, now, perhaps he gets a little pin-money on the side for cracking innocent persons on the head with an iron bar! His name's Colson, Brian Colson, and he works for *Zipp Brushes*, which has an office in Soho. Would you know the firm?"

"I know the firm," Roger said, heavily. He made no attempt to speak to Colson, but asked: "Can I see what was in his pockets?"

McClean brought everything on a tray—money in a cellophane bag, a wallet similarly packaged, keys, a handkerchief, some bus tickets, a comb; all of these things were bagged and labelled. In the wallet were some business cards, giving the Soho address of the brush firm, but no private address.

The man's clothes were of good quality, and he had thirty-nine pounds in notes in the wallet. He retained a clean-cut look, the air of a public school boy with a good games record; in spite of his smouldering resentment at being caught, his eyes were clear.

"He looks almost like an honest man, doesn't he?" said McClean, scoffingly. "Will you have us charge him here, or will you take him away, Mr. West?"

"I think we'll have him over at the Yard and charge him at Bow Street in the morning," Roger said. "The first thing to do is visit his employer." He glanced at Colson. "You can make it hard, or you can make it easy for yourself," he said. "Did the *Zipp* boss send you here?"

Colson didn't answer.

"Someone sent you to lie in wait for Anvill and me—was it your boss?"

There was no answer.

"It's a waste of time talking," declared McClean.

"It won't be a waste of time when we get him in dock on a charge of capital murder."

"Is Anvill dead, then?" McClean's voice rose up as if in surprise.

Colson's lips tightened, and alarm sparked in his eyes; but he did not speak or utter a sound.

Roger said: "Whatever you get paid for this, it won't be worth hanging. Keep that in mind." He turned away from the prisoner, knowing that he had not handled the situation well, and very conscious of his throbbing head and the fresh pain in his knee where he had twisted it. He wasn't fit enough to handle this job; that was an unpalatable fact.

He limped out of the cell, and the policeman-warder locked Colson in again; by the time the door was locked, the prisoner had sat down on a stiff-backed chair, and was staring straight ahead at a blank wall.

Along the passage, McClean said:

"It's none of my business, Mr. West, but you look as if you're out on your feet. You've got to be a fit man to work at your pace."

You had to be a fit man mentally and physically to do any kind of police work. That was the key factor, Roger thought savagely, and a lot of men were being made unfit for their job; almost certainly many more than he yet knew. And Anvill had made some discovery that he had wanted to talk about in secret, almost certainly about this case.

Roger said: "My trouble is night starvation. Can you fix me a sandwich?"

"Good heavens, man, are you hungry? I can soon cure that," said McClean warmly. "I'll have something sent up from the canteen. It will be a pleasure."

*   *   *   *   *

A doctor at Scotland Yard examined Roger's head wound, trimmed some more hair away, put on another dressing, and said: "You'll do, but don't get into any more fights." Roger left the First Aid Room and walked cautiously along to his office.

It was nearly three o'clock. He felt in an exasperating state of suspended animation; there was so much that he wanted to do quickly, and yet if he made a sudden movement his head threatened to lift from his shoulders. He went into his own office, and sat down. Cope, in his shirt sleeves, and with his tie hanging loose, said gruffly:

"What you need is a month's sick leave."

"What I need is the answer to this problem," Roger said. "Any word from Birwitz?"

"He says that Anvill told a sub-editor that he'd got a hot tip from a friend on another newspaper, and to hold space for tomorrow's front page," Cope said. "No one knows what the tip was."

"How's Anvill?"

"Half an hour ago, he was on the operating table—there's a brain injury, and it's touch and go." Cope slapped his desk with the flat of his hand. "You won't get any information out of him for a long time. We've two men standing by in case he should talk under the anaesthetic, but—" Cope broke off, gloomily.

"Those searches being made at Widderman's clubs?"

"Yes, right now."

"Did you get a message from Bow Street, to watch *Zipp* offices?"

Cope said: "Yes, the office is being watched, and I got a report in twenty minutes ago. Birwitz phoned in to say he'd reported this—he said you'd know what he meant."

"I know," Roger said heavily. Cope scratched the end of his nose. "Handsome, why don't you give that headache best, and go and let Janet kiss it better?"

"What was the report?"

Cope said: "You'll be crazy if you go over to those offices. You're not up to it."

"I can take my nurse with me. Give."

"I might have expected it," grumbled Cope. "All right, here it comes. Rocky Marlo went into the offices

half an hour ago. I gave word to have him picked up
if he left there before we went to see the big Bossman
there. The said Bossman is new. It's our James Kennedy,
all right."

"Anything fresh known?" asked Roger.

"No. We didn't know anything about *Zipp* until
Green became involved. There's nothing definite in
about Green, but one of our chaps said he thought he
saw him in the dining-room of the Regent Palace
yesterday."

"Make sure, will you?" urged Roger. "And I'll take
an Inspector and a couple of sergeants to *Zipp*." He
glanced up as the door opened, and an orderly came in
with some tea on a tray, and a large bottle of white
tablets beside it. "Doctor's orders." Roger said,
"Thanks." He waited until the door was closed,
wishing that his head would stop aching; the tablets
might help, but he felt pessimistic about that. "Have
you heard anything from the Assistant Commissioner
today?"

"There's some kind of conference," Cope said. "If
Hardy was here, he'd order you not to go out again."
After a pause, Cope went on grudgingly: "Birwitz is
back from Fleet Street. Want him on this job?"

"No. Send him to the Regent Palace Hotel. He
knows Green well enough to pick him out."

"Right," said Cope, and gave up trying to keep
Roger away from the offices of *Zipp*.

*   *   *   *   *

Roger saw two police cars parked within easy reach
of the narrow building in Dean Street where the brush
firm had its offices. He saw five plainclothesmen within
sight, too, and was quite sure that Rocky Marlo knew
that the premises were being watched—Birwitz had
'reported'. He saw six or seven smallish men, three of
them hatless, two of them with caps pulled very low
over their foreheads and the backs of their necks, and

wondered if these were the two of Marlo's men whose heads had been shaved.

As he stepped out of the car, a Yard detective-sergeant came hurrying forward and gave him a hand; nothing could have made it more obvious that he looked as if he needed help.

"Any problems?"

"Don't know yet, sir."

"Marlo still there?"

"Oh, yes," said the detective-sergeant. "We're watching back and front. He's still there, all right. And a lot of his boys have drifted this way, too." The sergeant was one of the older men at the Yard; hardy and tough. "I wouldn't put it past them to make trouble if we pick Rocky up."

"How many men have we got here?"

"Twelve in all."

"When I'm inside, get Mr. Cope on the radio and ask him to arrange for a squad of uniformed men from Marlborough Street to come and make themselves obvious, and we'll bring more of our own chaps, too."

The sergeant's eyes brightened.

"Right, sir! But—er—you're not going in there alone, are you?"

"No," said Roger. "Inspector Morris will come with me."

Morris was standing near the doorway of the building, and gave a knowing grin as Roger came up. The entrance to the offices was through the shop, and the shop itself was filled with brushes of all shapes and sizes, mostly packed in plastic containers or in printed boxes. The window had a wide selection of household brushes, too. In a corner a post card announced:

Door to Door Salesmen Required
Salary and Good Commission

"The offices are on the third floor," Morris said. His hair was iron grey, and grew upwards rather like a brush made of porcupine's quills; he had a brick-red face. "There's no lift."

"Like to carry me?" Roger asked.

Morris laughed dutifully.

As he went up the stairs, putting most of his weight on his right leg, Roger felt frustrated and angry with himself. Many of the victims of the anonymous letters must have approached a job feeling much the same; feeling, in fact, that they couldn't put their heart into their work. Was he being too stubborn? The thought slid out of his mind as quickly as it had flashed in.

He reached the half landing below the third floor, and heard voices coming from above him. The stairs were covered with coconut matting, and their footsteps made little sound, although they creaked sometimes. At a landing window, Roger looked out and saw a doorway opposite, with an archway made of photographs of semi-nude girls, neon blinking on and off, a simple announcement reading:

Girls, Girls, Girls!
Back to Nature

Below it, in much smaller lettering, was the legend:

The High-Lo Club

That was one of Widderman's.

Morris reached the door of the offices before Roger. He stood waiting. Inside, the men were still talking, but there was no doubt that they knew Roger and Morris were on the way. Marlo's men would have telephoned reports of every police move. Morris looked uncertain. Roger felt a tension greater than any he had known for a long time—because of what had happened to Anvill and to him. If Marlo decided to use violence, there was no telling where he would stop or how far he would go.

Roger said: "I'll knock."

He rapped sharply at the door, then tried the

handle; it turned freely. He pushed, and found that the door was not locked. The voices sounded more loudly, although there was a break in the conversation, as if the speakers were watching the door and had seen it move.

One man was saying:

"Well, if he takes over the Brighton area as well, he'll expect another all-over five per cent. Think it's worth it?" That was Rocky Marlo, whose voice was unmistakable, very hard, almost metallic.

The other man said: "If he gets the business, of course it's worth it."

That sounded so normal; but both men must be watching the door, must realise what was going to happen. Were they prepared to use violence? Was there someone else inside, ready to attack? Roger felt his heart beating fast as he pushed the door wider open.

Two men were standing in a small office, and the doors of two other offices stood open. Rocky Marlo was sideways to Roger, a man as hard as his name suggested, very broad, very powerful, craggy-featured. He had hair so black that in a man of nearing fifty it seemed obviously dyed. In a way, he reminded Roger of Widderman, but the likeness had never been apparent before. He turned his head as if with an effort, for his neck was so short. Bright light from the ceiling shimmered on his eyes.

The other man was taller, well-dressed, almost dapper; and Roger saw with a sense of foreboding that ex-Chief Inspector James Kennedy had not changed much. He looked now as he had in the old days; almost too smooth.

They must have known that the police were on the way; their conversation, even the way they were standing and talking, was obviously calculated for Roger's benefit; but they both stared at him as if they were completely surprised.

18

FACILITIES

ROCKY MARLO shifted his position so that he could look at Roger more squarely from his cloudy, dark brown eyes, and he said: "What do you want?"

Kennedy exclaimed, as if surprised: "It's West!"

"I don't need telling it's West," said Marlo, harshly. "Don't tell me he's come for a spare-time job."

Roger said: "You won't find it so funny when you're inside, Marlo." He looked at Kennedy, seeing his finely drawn features, the unmistakable likeness to his daughter, the well-cut clothes. "I'm looking for the General Manager of the *Zipp* Brush Company," he said.

"You're looking at him," said Kennedy. "How can I help you?"

Roger was reminded vividly of the way he had felt when he had seen Widderman; this man had the same secretive, almost mocking smile, accompanied by such precise courtesy and determination not to say a word out of place. These men were taking him for a ride. He knew it, yet couldn't prevent it—and he was too far short of his best to handle the situation properly.

"I'd like to see a complete list of your agents," he said. "Also some information about two of them in particular."

"Why?" demanded Kennedy.

"Because one of them is wanted for a charge of attempted murder which might become capital murder before the day is out."

"One of *my* men?" Kennedy pretended to be shocked; or else he was really shocked. "Who do you mean?"

"Don't take any notice of him," Marlo sneered. "He's trying to put the wind up you."

"Who's the man?" demanded Kennedy.

"His name is Colson."

"*Colson?*" Kennedy exclaimed.

Obviously that shook him badly, although he tried to cover it. It had an effect on Marlo, too, although not so severe. There was little doubt that Kennedy needed time to recover, so this was really bad news. The difficulty was to find the right follow-up.

"Why send him after Anvill?" Roger demanded. "It made you an accessory—"

"All right, West," Kennedy interrupted. "I know what it would make me, but I don't know what you're talking about." Now that they were over the initial shock, both he and Marlo seemed very sure of themselves; they certainly weren't behaving as if they were afraid of what the police might find here.

"I'd like some more information about Colson," Roger said.

"What you'd like and what you'll get is a different matter," Marlo jeered.

"Take it easy, Rocky," Kennedy protested. "If the police need help, we'd better give it to them." He raised his voice. "Rachel!"

There was a scraping of chair legs on the floor, the tap-tap-tap of heels, and then a blonde appeared in one of the doorways, so huge-bosomed that she did not seem to be real. She was nice-looking, and had an exceptionally good complexion; her make-up wasn't overdone although she wore plenty of lipstick. Her eyes were a beautiful cornflower blue. She looked as ingenuous as Kennedy, as if she was deliberately acting the dumb blonde.

"Did you want me, Mr. Kennedy?"

"Yes, Rachel—get Brian Colson's file, will you?" Kennedy turned to Roger. "Who was the other chap you're interested in?"

"Horace Green."

"Your chaps had a look at Green's file earlier in the

week," said Kennedy, and shrugged. "But if that's what you want that's what you'd better have. Get a move on, sweetie!" He seemed to have recovered completely.

The girl turned, with a flouncing of wide skirts which were so short that she looked a little ridiculous; or would have done but for the slender beauty of her legs. She disappeared.

Marlo took out a fat gold cigarette case, put a cigarette to his lips, and said:

"I'll be getting along, Jim."

"Okay, Rocky."

"And okay for Percy and Brighton?"

"Give him a month's trial."

"Okay, Jim."

"Okay, Rocky."

It was a challenge, of course, calculated and well-timed. If Rocky were stopped, there was a risk that his men outside would start a rough-house; if he were allowed to go, it would look as if he had been able to cock a snook at the police. He sneered at Roger as he moved towards the door, while Morris stood very still, in his way.

"Marlo," Roger said.

"I'm busy, copper."

"*Mister* Marlo," said Roger, mildly, "you'll have plenty of time to kick your heels in jail if you're not very careful. Someone is taking you for a ride."

Marlo exclaimed: "Taking *me* for a ride!"

"That's right."

"Don't make me laugh," Marlo said, but he stood where he was, and for the first time looked uneasy; this wasn't the kind of approach that he had expected. "I've gotta date—"

"You've got a date at the Yard, with me."

"Don't you believe it!"

"Listen, Marlo," Roger said, "you can tell your crowd of chop-men and razor boys that they can go

home and get their heads shaved. I've forty men
within sight of this place, and your mob will be written
off if you make me move in. Open a window, shout down
and tell them to make themselves scarce, then come
along with me without making a fuss."

Marlo was breathing heavily.

"Give me one good reason."

"If you want another reason, here it is," said Roger.
"You've got a lot of enemies. Some of them are lodging
information against you which might or might not be
true. I'm giving you a chance to answer questions, and
if your answers seem straight, you'll be able to go home
and find out who's slandering you."

"Who's lying about me?"

"Friends and old business acquaintances," Roger
said.

"*Widderman?*"

"I can't stop you guessing."

"If it's Widderman—"

"Listen, Rocky," said Kennedy, and he sounded
anxious. "If I were you I'd do what West advises. We
don't want trouble now." He turned from Rocky to
Roger, and went on in a voice which was as persuasive
as Widderman's had been: "Mr. West, Marlo's got a
bad reputation, and everybody knows it, but it's not
justified. These men you call razor boys and chop-men
are ordinary, decent chaps, and they nearly all work for
me. They spend their spare time in this district, but that
doesn't make them criminals. I know as much as you do
about the law, and I tell you that Rocky's got nothing to
worry about. There isn't a thing you can fix on to him."

"And there won't be, either," Marlo insisted. He
sneered again: "Okay, I'll be a good boy." He went
to the window, flung it up, and leaned out; he waved
and shouted, and Roger could imagine every policeman
down in the street waiting now for the coming attack.
"Okay, pals!" called Marlo. "There's no more business
today, you can all scram. See you later."

He waved again.

There was a roar from below, a derisive-sounding laughter; the mood of the men could not be mistaken. Morris, close to Roger's side, whispered: "I don't like this." Rachel flounced out, holding the two files, and as she walked towards Roger she was simpering, as if she also shared the joke. Only Kennedy looked serious, as he stopped the girl.

"All right, I'll have them."

"Very good, Mr. Kennedy," the girl said primly.

More laughter was floating up from the street, and Rocky Marlo was still at the window, leaning out. When he glanced round, he was grinning broadly; slyly. Kennedy took the folders, and the girl turned round and went flouncing back, her bottom looking enormous in the flared skirt, her legs unbelievably creamy and trim.

"Here are the two records," Kennedy said. "I hope that Colson isn't really in trouble."

"He's in trouble," Roger said heavily, and took the files. "Thanks. How many typewriters have you here, Mr. Kennedy?"

"Three—or is it four? Rachel!"

The girl turned in the doorway.

"How many typewriters have we got?"

"Well, we've got the old Underwood that ought to be on the scrap heap, I've always told you, and then we've the Olympia, and the two Remingtons, including the portable."

"A Remington portable?" demanded Roger.

"Oh, yes. Would you like to see it?"

"Yes, please."

It was a semi-standard portable, and the type size was quite different from the Olivetti on which the poison pen letters were typed. By the time Roger had finished checking, Rocky Marlo had come back, and the laughter from the street had stopped.

"Okay, I'll come quietly," Rocky said.

For some reason the whole situation now amused him; it was as if he and Kennedy, as well as Widderman and his secretary, were throwing up a kind of smoke-screen in their determination to fool the police. Morris was standing by the landing door, obviously prepared for any kind of trick.

"You go ahead," Roger said. "We'll follow."

"Right."

"Mind you don't fall," jeered Rocky, and gave a harsh laugh as if he were really amused. He did not need telling to follow Morris, and Roger brought up the rear, still wary, not convinced that it was going to be as easy as this. He remembered that on the two occasions when there had been danger it had come without warning; the fact that it seemed so imminent now probably meant that none was there.

A door opened, at the foot of the stairs; a girl appeared, blonde but skinny, and wearing a hospital mask of gauze. The sight of her so startled Morris that he missed a step, and Marlo almost banged into him. Roger, on the landing above, saw the girl toss something into the air, and disappear, slamming the door.

"Look out!" roared Morris.

He leapt upwards, as if trying to intercept whatever the girl had thrown, but he missed. It was small and round, and looked rather like a firework banger. Rocky covered his eyes with his arm. Roger did the same thing, instinctively, then heard a plop and a dull explosion, not heavy enough to cause even momentary alarm. Roger opened his eyes. Smoke was streaming from a little container which lay on the stairs between him and Marlo, smoke so thick and black that it could only come from a smoke-bomb.

"Don't move, Marlo!" Roger went down half a dozen stairs quickly, ready to grapple with the man, but Marlo made no attempt to get away. The smoke was billowing out in great clouds, and Morris was beating the air about his head, as if to try to disperse it.

Roger heard another plop, followed by another explosion; he felt sure that the smoke-bomb had come from above, from Kennedy or the girl, but would never be able to swear to it, for the bomb was hidden in the pall from the first one.

Morris reached the street door, and flung it open.

"Don't try any tricks, Marlo," he said thickly. Roger saw his broad frame in the doorway, as if he were going to make sure that Marlo did not have a chance to get away. But Marlo made no attempt to, and as they stood there with the smoke getting thicker and thicker, and beginning to stink as well as to catch at their throats, there was a shout of alarm from the street. Roger saw two or three women scurrying, heard a police whistle, and wanted to push past Marlo, but there was no room in the narrow passage. Morris spun round. More women were running, and then Roger saw the cloud of smoke outside, and realised what had happened; smoke-bombs were being released out there as well as in the building.

Marlo was still standing in the doorway; when Roger reached him, he turned round, grinning broadly.

"What a stink," he said, in that hard, metallic-sounding voice. "Just right for stinkers!"

More smoke was blowing and billowing in the street, a crowd of twenty or thirty people appeared, and Roger saw several of the Yard men driven back by the evil-smelling vapour. Now Morris was beginning to choke, Marlo kept coughing, and from behind Roger on the stairs Kennedy said in a grating voice:

"What's happening down there? What the hell's happening?"

Rocky Marlo gasped: "Don't ask *me*!" He swung round on Morris, and roared: "Why the hell don't you shut the door? We won't be able to see in front of our noses in a minute!"

Roger said: "All right, Marlo, we'll be back for you." He pushed past, into the street, with Morris, who

slammed the door on their backs. The whirling smoke
writhed and eddied in and out of shop doorways; men
and women were choking as they closed windows and
shut doors. Police were coughing as they tried to breathe,
some rolling helplessly against the shop fronts. Apart
from the police and the shopkeepers, the street was now
clear of people. All of Rocky Marlo's men had gone, the
girls had gone, there were only the innocent passers-by,
and the police—and, some way off, people laughing
shrilly, almost hysterically.

Morris said furiously: "They're just making fools of
us. That's all they're doing."

"That's plenty," Roger wheezed; and began to
cough again.

Then he saw two cameras, large ones, set up in the
windows of nearby houses, and knew that the whole
scene had been photographed for cinema or television.

*   *   *   *   *

Two news-reel producers and both television groups
said the same thing; they had been tipped by telephone that the police were going to raid some Soho
premises, but they could not name their informants.
Obviously the information had been given as soon as
Birwitz had reported the likelihood of a raid on *Zipp*.
There had been plenty of time to make the arrangements, and smoke-bombs were easy to come by.

It had been very slick; like everything about the case.

19

BLACK MORNING

ROGER woke next morning with a dull ache over his
eyes, and wheeziness in his chest; all last evening he had
smelt the stink of the smoke in his nostrils, and it hadn't

gone yet. He sensed that he was alone. It was Saturday, never a slack day and yet one where the pressures sometimes eased; on Saturdays Janet would sometimes 'forget' to wake him.

He lay on his side, looking at bright sunlight through his lashes, and recalling everything that had happened in Soho, as well as the long interview he had had with Rocky Marlo afterwards. Marlo had repeated what Kennedy had said in the *Zipp* office, and, at half past nine, Roger had let him go back to his apartment over another, smaller club—one of the nastiest in the district, but which never actually broke the law when the police were around.

Between that time and midnight, Roger had taken report after report, of the fiasco in Dean Street, the effect of the smoke-bombs, the activities of the brush salesmen. He had talked to Birwitz on the telephone, and Birwitz had received no further instructions from anyone. Roger had seen Hardy, who had come back to the Yard late in the evening; Hardy said that the Commissioner had simply confirmed his, Hardy's, instructions, but he could not hide the fact that the burden of the responsibility was greater than ever.

There was no report of the Olivetti typewriter having been found.

Roger heard the stairs creak, listened intently, heard the sound again and guessed that Janet was coming quietly up the stairs. He had not taken the trouble to see what time it was, but as he hadn't come home until well after one-thirty, that wasn't important; Cope or Hardy would call him in emergency. He turned on his back, hitched himself up on his pillows, and put on a bright, broad smile as the door opened stealthily. He saw Janet's hand on it, the nicely shaped nails with their pink varnish; then her wavy hair. She peered in, cautiously, as if afraid that her breathing would wake him.

"*Boo!*" barked Roger.

Janet jumped. "You brute!"

"Didn't you know I had Hawk-Eye's ability to see through door panels?" asked Roger, and hitched himself further up. There was no need to depress Janet, and if he could work himself into a fairly bright mood, it might help him. "What's the time?"

"Just on ten o'clock."

"My God, I'll get the sack!"

"I half wish you would," said Janet.

The way she said that puzzled him, and now that he thought about her, her reaction to his 'boo' had been less spontaneous than it might have been. She wasn't smiling—in fact was very nearly frowning.

"Now what?" he demanded, warily.

"The newspapers ought to be put on a bonfire," Janet declared angrily, and her eyes sparkled and her cheeks flushed.

"So they've been at it, have they?"

"They're dreadful."

"Making me out the Yard's thickest head?"

"Making out the Yard—" Janet began, and then turned towards the door and said: "You'd better see them." She stepped on to the landing, and there was a sharp note in her voice when she called: "Boys!"

Roger judged the boys' mood when they answered meekly, and in unison: "Yes, Mum?"

"Bring the tea, and bring the papers."

"Right, Mum." That was Richard, and it was like Richard to add: "Don't take any notice of the slobs, Dad—no one with any sense will."

There were footsteps and muttered voices, while Janet came back from the door, then quite suddenly dropped on to the side of the double bed, and buried her face against Roger's shoulder. He sensed that she was very near to tears; she gave two or three convulsive sobs, and he felt the tension of her hands as she gripped his shoulders. He did not move, except to put his hands to the back of her head and to smooth her hair down, but he was beginning to feel alarmed. How bad could the stories be?

There was the chink of cups on a tray.

Janet pushed herself away from him. Tears were quivering on her eye-lashes but none had fallen.

"Oh, I'm a fool," she said crossly. "I don't want the boys to see me like this." She scurried across to the dressing-table, dabbing at her eyes. "It's so unfair."

"Unfair's one word," said Martin-called-Scoopy, from the landing. He came in with four morning newspapers. Roger saw the photographs on the front pages, and guessed at once what they were. From behind Martin came Richard, carrying the tea-tray.

"They're a lot of swine," Richard declared.

In spite of his tone, in spite of Janet standing with her back to them, in spite of Scoop's scowl, Roger felt a sudden impulse to laugh, and could not keep it back. Janet spun round, Richard gaped from the doorway, Scoop put his head on one side; he was always quick to see the funny side of any situation, and suddenly began to smile.

"*I'd* like to know what's funny," Janet cried.

"Anything in the newspapers which can make the family fuss me like this is quite all right with me," Roger declared. "It can't be as bad as that!"

"Oh, can't it?" barked Janet, her annoyance switched to him. "Well, look for yourself." Scoop brought the newspapers and spread them over the bed in front of Roger, arranging them with great care so that all four front page headlines and the pictures were visible.

The headlines screamed:

SOHO RIOT
POLICE SMOKED OUT
VICE RAID GOES UP IN SMOKE
ABORTIVE POLICE RAID IN SOHO

The pictures showed the people running, the police

beating at the smoke, 'girls' at the windows above the smoke sitting and grinning at the discomfiture of the police. It had been even more cunningly arranged than Roger had realised; and as he looked from one picture to another, he began to grin again. Martin glanced across at Janet, and winked. Richard put the tea-tray down on the bedside table, began to pour and said airily:

"Well, if that's all it does to you, it's okay with me."

"I can't understand what's got into you," Janet said, in vexation.

"Imagine what this would look like if I wasn't a policeman," Roger said. "The police stage what can easily be taken for a big vice raid, and all the ladies of easy virtue sit at their windows and have a good hearty laugh while the cops beat the smoke as if at a swarm of bees. Wouldn't *you* laugh?"

"But you *are* a policeman!"

Roger said half-ruefully: "I thought I was!" He took a cup of steaming tea. "Thanks, Fish," he went on absently, and as he sipped began to read the stories. All inclination to laugh soon faded, for three were written in highly critical tone about the Metropolitan Police Force.

The *Echo* read:

There are indications that the Home Secretary and the Commissioner of the Metropolitan Police are becoming increasingly worried about the condition of this once great Force. Stories of corruption are on the increase. Cases are being lost by the police because the cases for the prosecution are inadequately prepared, or should never have been brought. An officer such as Detective Constable Birwitz makes a savage attack on a prisoner, and is restored to duty after the most cursory inquiry, apparently at the instigation of Superintendent Roger West.

The *Echo* believes that it is time for a full inquiry to be made into the operation of the Force. It may be that methods and organisation sufficient for the situation twenty years ago, are now hopelessly inadequate. It may be that haphazard recruiting has weakened the Force dangerously. It may be that Superintendent West, and those engaged in last night's fiasco, are relying too much on their reputation and the Scotland Yard tradition.

Whatever the cause, the good name of the police has never been so gravely challenged—and very few criminals have ever had it so good.

We believe that all responsible citizens will support our demand for a full inquiry, and we ask that it be started at once and given a limited time in which to report its finding. The matter is extremely urgent.

Jane, watching Roger, moved away from the dressing-table and said quietly: "So it isn't so funny."

"Just about what we expected," Roger replied gruffly. He scanned the next two papers, and picked up the *Globe*. "Is this still friendly?"

"Fairly, but it's more concerned with the attack on its own reporter than it is about the situation."

"Anvill," Roger said, heavily. "Any news of him?"

After an awkward pause, Martin said: "Yes, Dad. Mr. Cope rang up, and said that he died during the night. And Mr. Hardy rang up, too. He said we weren't to disturb you, but as soon as you were up, he would like to see you at his office."

After a long pause, Roger said: "It's time I was on my way. Twenty minutes, Jan?" He pushed the bed-clothes back and jumped out of bed, touching the floor as Janet exclaimed: "Be careful!" He landed too heavily, and winced, but the pain wasn't bad, and he laughed a little gruffly, and went to the bathroom.

* * * * *

Earlier that morning, Meg Birwitz fetched the newspapers from the front door, knowing that Witzy was anxious to see them; he was in the bathroom, shaving. She went in, and he glanced round, then swung round and snatched the papers. With one side of his face smothered with lather like cumulus cloud, he scanned the headlines and the story. They took three newspapers, including the *Globe*.

"Now I really would like to break some necks," Birwitz said savagely.

"I suppose it was inevitable that they should pick on Superintendent West," Meg reflected.

"They had to find a scapegoat, and he was handy," growled Birwitz. "And they were bound to have another crack at me."

"Witzy—"

"Yes?"

"Witzy, are you sure that you're doing the wise thing?"

"I'm doing what West wants, isn't that good enough?"

After a pause, Meg said: "I don't know. I must go and see to that bacon." She turned and hurried out, while Birwitz stared after her for a long time. He finished shaving, washed, and strode into the kitchen before he had put on his shirt. The bacon was keeping warm over the grill, and Meg was cutting bread for toast.

"Meg, what's on your mind?" Birwitz demanded.

"Oh, forget it."

"Don't be daft. What's on your mind? What made you say 'I don't know' and look like that?"

"You did," Meg answered, and turned to face him. "Witzy, you said yourself that there had to be a scapegoat. Supposing this gets worse. Supposing Mr. West's plans fail, and *he* needs a scapegoat. You're giving information away to these criminals, and—well, who else knows that you're doing it on his orders?"

"Damn it, Meg, you're talking about a superintendent at the Yard!"

"I'm talking about a man who's going to be in serious trouble if he's not very careful," Meg said, and she moved forward with her hands outstretched. "Darling, don't you see? Oh, I like him, I don't think he would let you down for the sake of it, but if it becomes a question of your future or his—"

"Let's get this straight," Birwitz said. "What you're suggesting is that West might deny that he gave me these orders, so that I would be blamed for selling information."

"It *could* work out like that, couldn't it?" Meg was almost pleading.

"I suppose it could," conceded Birwitz, slowly. "Yes, I suppose it could, but I don't believe it ever would. A man in West's position—"

"Senior officers have been corrupted before. How do you know that behind that pleasant smile and that friendly manner he *isn't* selling the Yard out?"

Birwitz said: "How do I *know*? If it comes to that, how do you know that I'm not?" He gave a laugh which had no humour in it. "Forget it, Meg, it's silly nonsense. If you keep at it, you'll put me off my breakfast."

"I only hope you're right, Witzy. Where are you going this morning?"

"To the Regent Palace, where the man Green was seen," said Birwitz. "If I'm wanted, West will find me there. I'll just go and put a shirt on."

* * * * *

Horace Green came out of the bathroom at the hotel, and stopped short. Betty was half-way between the bed and the door, bending down with one hand outstretched towards the newspaper which had been pushed beneath the door. She was stark naked and her pale body was quite, quite beautiful, the skin so smooth, the curves so gentle and yet seductive. She sensed that Horace was near, and turned to glance at him, laughing as if she were delighted at being caught out, then straightened up and held her arms out to him.

"Betty, you're so lovely it hurts to see you," he said hoarsely, and he slid his arms round her and crushed her against him. "If anything should happen to you, I'd kill whoever did it, and I'd kill myself afterwards."

"Don't talk like that," Betty protested. She forced herself away from him, but not completely free, and stared into his face. "Don't talk like that," she repeated fiercely. "I couldn't bear to lose you, I didn't realise how much I loved you until—until this happened. I'd do anything for you, absolutely anything!"

He pulled her close to him again, and began to kiss her passionately, to caress her, to surrender to her as completely as she surrendered to him.

It was an hour later when he got out of bed again, slid his arms into a dressing-gown, and picked up the newspapers. Then he telephoned for room service, sat on the edge of his bed, and unfolded the *Echo*. His eyes rounded, his mouth formed a big O.

"What is it?" Betty demanded quickly. "What is it, darling?"

"You take an eyeful of this," said Green. "Caw, strewth!" His eyes glistened as he read. "It happened just outside the brush company's place, too—look, there's Rocky Marlo at that top window, and Kennedy with him. Marlo's laughing all over his ugly dial!"

He studied the photographs.

"There's Handsome West," he declared, pointing. "What a smack in the eye for a copper! I feel almost sorry for him. I know one thing, Betty, it's a good thing we're out of it. Know what I think? I think we ought to get out of here today and go somewhere the police won't expect to find me. Marlo's got plenty on his hands, he won't worry me now. How about Bournemouth? It's posher there than Brighton, and further away from London. How does it sound?"

"If it's okay with you," said Betty simply, "it's okay with me."

"We'll have breakfast here," decided Green, "and then I'll go and pay the bill, while you're packing. Think you can pack all by yourself?"

"I can pack," Betty said drily. "I can do a lot of things!"

Half an hour later, Horace Green stepped out of the room, glanced right and left along the passage, saw a middle-aged maid entering one of the bedrooms, but no one else in sight. He closed the door, and heard Betty shoot the bolt, behind him; he wasn't taking the slightest chances with Betty. Although they had hidden out safely here, he knew that the danger was as great as ever; he could give evidence against Rocky Marlo which was exactly what the police wanted—and his life wouldn't be worth a throw of the dice if Rocky thought that he would squeal to the police. But if he read the signs aright the police were after Rocky, so his evidence might never be needed. Then he could come into the open again, and have nothing to worry about.

He passed a bedroom with its door wide open, so that he could see the rumpled bedclothes, a breakfast tray piled up with dirty crockery, orange peel and apple peelings, and although he saw a movement inside the room, he did not give it a second thought. He was half-way between the room and the corner which led to the lifts when he heard a sound behind him, and it came so suddenly that he turned quickly on his heel.

He cried: "*No!*"

He flung out his arms, to try to defend himself, but had no chance at all. He felt the searing pain of the knife burying itself in his vitals, and died.

20

CAUSE FOR SUSPICION

BIRWITZ stood in front of Roger's desk, later that Saturday morning, his face set, his eyes narrowed, and touched with the shock of what had happened. Roger was talking on the telephone while looking up at the man from Richmond. The caller was Hardy, asking for the latest information:

"Yes, it was Horace Green, and he died instantly," Roger reported. "There are some stories of a man dressed like a workman and carrying a bag of electrician's tools seen on that floor, but there's no confirmation. . . . Yes, Birwitz was downstairs at the hotel when it happened, watching the stairs and the lift as instructed. . . . Yes, he's with me now . . . Yes, the widow's all right."

There was a longer pause.

"Right," said Roger into the telephone. He put the receiver down, pushed his chair back, and looked up into the younger man's face. Birwitz stood like a man on parade. It was difficult even to begin to guess what was going on in his mind but obviously this had been a severe shock to him, and doubts about the wisdom of using a man whose nerves had been in such a raw state for so long were crowding in on Roger.

Roger said: "You say Green's wife collapsed?"

"Flat out, sir."

"Did she make any statement at all?"

"In between her screaming she said that he'd intended to leave for Bournmouth today, but apart from that I couldn't get any sense out of her, and the doctor insisted on giving her a sedative."

"When is she likely to be able to talk?"

"Some time this afternoon at the earliest, the doctor says."

"That will have to do. Was anything found in Green's room?"

"Nothing at all of any use to us, sir. Your officers came and made the search, of course. I simply took their instructions."

"Any idea why Green should be murdered?"

"Only one, sir."

"Tell me."

"Because he could have put a finger on Rocky Marlo. Or—"

"Or?"

"Whoever is behind it."

"Yes," said Roger. "Rocky Marlo, Kennedy, Widderman—I should think it's bound to be one of those three. You've had a chance to study all the evidence, Birwitz. What do you think of it?"

"It could be any one of them, or all three of them together," Birwitz said, and his eyes seemed to brighten. "Someone's setting out to make us look a lot of bloody fools, there can't be any more doubt about that."

Roger was thinking: "He's got a good, clear mind, I wonder what's worrying him now, apart from another sense of failure." He knew that that might be the explanation of Birwitz's tension. Aloud, he asked: "Did this morning's newspapers worry you?"

"They got under my skin a bit."

"They got under my wife's," Roger said drily.

Birwitz's eyes seemed to brighten again. "They worried my wife, too." He moistened his lips, and his body seemed to sway forward as if to get nearer the desk. "I've learned one thing from all this, whatever comes of it. If I ever have a kind of under-cover job in future I won't tell my wife. She—" He gulped, raised his right hand, and reminded Roger of young Richard more than of Martin. "As a matter of fact she got a queer notion in her head that if things got any worse, you might use me as a scapegoat. She—I told her it was crazy but she wouldn't listen."

Roger said soberly: "No, I don't suppose she would." He pondered. "You mean she wonders if I'll deny giving you the instructions to fix these leakages of information."

"Yes, sir."

Roger grinned. "Well, it may not help much with your wife, but you needn't worry. A full report of what I've done has been lodged with the Assistant Commissioner, and I wasn't thinking of my own frailty. I did think that if someone crowned me with an iron bar or pushed me under a bus, you wouldn't have a leg to stand on. You can forget that possibility."

Birwitz drew a deep breath, but didn't speak.

"Now let's plan the next leakage," Roger went on. "You can say that I'm going around like a raging demon, that there's conference after conference at the Yard, and we don't know where to turn next. We're pretty sure our man is Marlo but we think that Kennedy may be involved, and we aren't really convinced that Widderman's in the clear. Let them get a kick out of our frustration, but let them know they're all suspected. That clear?"

"Yes, sir."

"All these messages have been passed on by telephone so far, haven't they?"

"Yes."

"If you get half a chance to meet anyone on the other side, take it."

"I will," promised Birwitz. He looked younger and quite himself; a man with a big load off his mind. "I can't help blaming myself for what happened to Green. If I'd found him by searching the bedrooms instead of watching the lifts and staircases—"

"You did what you were told to do," Roger said briskly. "If we all blamed ourselves for that kind of miscalculation, we'd be so busy condemning ourselves that we would never get a job done. Report in whenever you can."

"Right, sir." Birwitz clicked his heels, and turned off smartly.

When the door closed on him, Roger smiled faintly, and was glad to have anything to smile about.

Then Cope came in, looking thoroughly dejected. He stood disconsolately at the window for a few minutes, while Roger made notes. When Cope turned round, he said:

"I've been at the Yard twenty-seven years, Handsome, and I've never known the chaps more fed up."

"Can't say I blame them," said Roger, drily. "They want more to do, that's probably the trouble!" He won a scowl, not a grin. "We haven't found any kind of connection between the solicitors who've won cases against us, all the accused who've got off don't seem to be associated with one another. Nothing makes sense except that someone is trying to break down police morale, and takes every chance of doing it. We need that Olivetti typewriter more urgently than anything else and we haven't any idea where it is," he said. "I sometimes wish I was still a detective sergeant. When is Radlett due to report?"

"One o'clock," answered Cope. "He's coming in this morning, I told him to make sure he had everything ready for a detailed report."

"I'll see him," Roger said.

"What's on your mind?"

"That typewriter," Roger said.

*   *   *   *   *

Radlett still looked under the regulation height of five feet eight inches, and although he was wearing a well-pressed suit instead of blazer and flannels, and showed none of the rather over-breezy air that he had when canvassing for *Zipp* brushes, he looked nothing like a policeman. He came briskly into Roger's office a little before one o'clock, obviously expectantly.

"Hallo, Radlett," Roger said. "What have you got for us?"

"Damn all," announced Radlett. "Sorry, sir."

"Drawn a complete blank?"

"I've sold a few brushes and earned a few quid, and I've done everything I've been told," said Radlett. "I was at a weekly salesman's conference this morning, they don't do a lot of Saturday work, and met twenty or so of the other salesmen. Most of them seem to make a fairly good thing out of it. They each have a sample case, they carry a few of the more popular brushes

round with them for cash sales, but most of the orders
are delivered the following day—all cash against
delivery. It's a good can't-lose business, Mr. West."

"You mean, for the firm?"

"I don't think the men do badly."

"Any indication that any of them do too well?"

"I don't know them well enough to be sure yet,"
said Radlett. "Two or three of them flash their money
about, but they do a lot of betting, and it wouldn't
surprise me if they pick up quite a lot of ready money
at the dogs."

"How often do you meet other salesmen?"

"Not very often," Radlett answered. "We bump into
each other occasionally, and there are a few cafés
where they sometimes meet after the day's work, to
exchange notes. Everyone has to report in to the head
office by telephone once a day, to pick up any postal
requests for a call or for brushes. It's very well
organised."

"Organised and prosperous," Roger remarked
thoughtfully. "Who do you talk to when you report in?"

"Kennedy or Marlo."

"So Marlo really does a job for the firm."

"He works all right," asserted Radlett. "If a salesman needs brushes for an urgent delivery, Marlo will
often take them out to the district. If I had to report on
what I've seen so far, Mr. West, I would have to say
that it's a wholly genuine business. On the other hand
I haven't been in it long, and they may not have started
to let me into any of the secrets. I know one thing for
sure."

"What's that?"

"The easiest thing in the world to get into a house to
demonstrate the brushes," said Radlett, and grinned.
"Some women give you a gusty 'no' and slam the door
in your face, but a lot of them are ready to give you a
cuppa. The best times are from eleven to half past in
the morning, between clearing up and getting the

midday meal, and from three o'clock to four in the afternoon. They seem to be slacker then."

"They?"

"Housewives. About one in a dozen seems ready for a bit of extra-marital, if you know what I mean."

Roger said: "And it's really easy to case the joints?"

"No trouble at all, Mr. West. As a matter of fact you get an idea the moment you look in through the front window. If the furniture's all right and there's a decent piano and one or two good pictures, you know you're on the way. If the housewife herself opens the door, as they usually do these days, you can see if there's money from the rings she wears, or her ear-rings, or her clothes. If I were casing these places to report to someone for burgling or breaking-in, I could point out the most profitable houses in five minutes."

Roger said: "I wish we'd been able to talk to Green."

"Our Horace?" Radlett laughed. "He's quite a character, from all accounts. He looks meek and mild, but if anyone tries to put anything across him, he—"

"Hits back, and gets murdered," Roger interrupted.

Radlett caught his breath. "Horace Green?"

"Yes."

"So they got him," Radlett said, slowly and heavily. He lost his perkiness all of a sudden, thrust his right hand into his pocket, took out a packet of cigarettes, and hesitated. Roger waved to him to light up. "Poor devil. When?"

"This morning," Roger answered. "And you probably know that Anvill of the *Globe* died."

"Yes," said Radlett, and drew deeply on the cigarette. The news of Green's death had obviously upset him, and he began to move about, restricting his movements only because of Roger. "I don't know if you think the same as I do, sir."

"What's that?"

"We must be getting close—closer than we realised, perhaps. They wouldn't kill for the sake of it. This man

Colson, who killed Anvill, isn't very popular with the
other men. He joined about six months ago, and they
soon gave him one of the best districts, where money's
pretty easy to come by."

"Favouritism," Roger remarked thoughtfully. "We
need to find out why." He stopped speaking, looked at
Radlett very frankly, stood up, and said: "Well, you
know the strength of it, Radlett. They'll kill if they
think it will help them."

"And if they discovered who I was they would
probably cut my throat too," said Radlett. He didn't
smile or make light of it, but sounded quite composed as
he went on: "It's one of the unavoidable risks, sir."

"Yes. And I want you to take another one which
isn't unavoidable."

Radlett said, slowly, warily: "Do you?"

"But it's not an order."

"What is it, sir?"

"We haven't found that typewriter," Roger told
him, "and we need it more than ever. There are four
places where we haven't looked. We might get search
warrants for two, but we certainly couldn't for the
others. We've no grounds for applying, and if we asked
for search warrants without full justification, and the
Press found out—"

"Wow!" exclaimed Radlett. "Where are the places?"

"One is Kennedy's home. One is Widderman's
home. One is Muriel Kennedy's flat. The fourth is
Marlo's flat. If it's easy to get into homes as a brush
salesman—" he broke off.

Radlett said: "I see what you mean." He stubbed out
the half-smoked cigarette and immediately lit another.
"Yes, I see what you mean." He drew in smoke deeply,
let it out, and said deliberately: "I'll have a go."

"I'll say again that you don't have to."

"I'll have a go, sir," repeated Radlett. "But there's
just one thing."

"Yes?"

"If I am caught in the act, you'll back me up, won't you?"

Very slowly, almost painfully, Roger said: "Yes, fully." He felt frightened by the question—or rather, by the fact that Radlett thought the question necessary. First Birwitz's wife, then to a degree, Birwitz himself, and now Radlett. Once the members of the Force began to wonder whether they could trust one another, once senior officers were suspected of double-dealing, the situation would be about as bad as it could be. He had not realised how far the poison had spread.

The letter about Hardy and the letter to Hardy were all part of the same pattern.

"Then I'll be glad to have a go," Radlett said. "It will have to be Monday, though. If *Zipp* salesmen were to call on Saturday afternoon or a week-end, they'd be known as phoneys before they started."

"Make it Monday," decided Roger. "That will give us all time to digest the stories that the Sunday newspapers regale us with. Thanks, Radlett."

Radlett grinned suddenly. "I think I'm glad of the chance, sir." He went out, smartly, and Cope looked up from his desk, smiling twistedly, and after a long pause, said knowingly:

"So you wish you were a sergeant, too. Rather do this job than let Radlett do it, I suppose."

"Wouldn't you?"

"I suppose you're right," said Cope. "But you and me are getting too long in the tooth for that kind of lark. I hope they give us a quiet week-end. I promised my kids I'd take them round Hampton Court."

*   *   *   *   *

Martin said to Roger, on the Sunday afternoon, while Janet was cooking crumpets in front of the coal fire in the front room:

"Let's leave the scholarship idea for a bit, Dad. You've got plenty on your mind."

"After all, you don't want to make a decision and then regret it," Richard remarked sagely.

Roger cocked an eye.

"You mean I don't want to say 'no' and make Scoop wish I'd said 'yes'." He contemplated Janet, as she sat flushed and attractive on a pouffe, with a crumpet on a toasting fork; they had discussed this at some length the previous night and knew exactly what the answer would be. "It's your mother's fault, really," he said. "She bullied me into saying 'have a go'." He thought of Radlett as he used that phrase.

Martin jumped up: "You mean it? I can try?"

"It had better be a damned good try."

"Yip-yip-yip-*yippee*!" cried Richard, outwardly much more excited than his brother. Martin was looking steadily into Roger's eyes, while Janet twisted round to watch them, the firelight shining on her hair.

"Thanks, Dad," Martin said, very quietly, and then looked round at his mother. "Thanks, Mum."

"Don't thank me yet," retorted Janet. "I want one of the family to be smart enough to avoid going into the police force, and this seems the only way."

* * * * *

Having Radlett get into those homes seemed the only way, too.

Radlett was on Roger's mind a great deal that weekend. He kept picturing the body of Horace Green, and the wound on Anvill's head—and his own wound, which could so easily have been much worse.

21

THE TYPEWRITER

"No, we certainly don't want any brushes here," said the middle-aged woman who answered Radlett's call at Kennedy's home. "You didn't say *Zipp*, did you?"

"Yes, and I assure you that—"

The woman interrupted laughingly: "You don't know what a joke that is! I work for the owner of *Zipp*!" She waited for Radlett to respond to that remarkable coincidence, and after a moment of pretended astonishment, he chuckled as if quite naturally.

"Well I'm blowed! You mean, Mr. Kennedy?"

"That's right, Mr. Jim Kennedy."

"You'd better not tell him I called here," said Radlett, anxiously.

"Don't you worry, he would say that it was proof you were doing a good job," declared the woman. "Not that I would worry him with it just now, Mrs. Kennedy's trouble is quite enough for him at the moment." She was one of the garrulous ones, Radlett realised already, but so far she had kept him at the front door, and he was wondering anxiously what excuse he could make to get inside. It was eleven o'clock, and she was the type who might well offer him tea or coffee. "Mrs. Kennedy's son has had a serious accident, apparently she's ever so upset," she went on.

"What kind of accident?" asked Radlett, as much to prolong the conversation as anything.

"To tell you the truth, I don't really know," the woman said. "The son doesn't live here, she only heard about it by telephone—last Friday, it was. I was here when she was told. I thought she was going mad, and she had such a row with—but I mustn't stand here gossiping!"

Radlett said: "I'm sorry about that trouble, but I can understand, though. I had a nasty car accident myself a year ago. Well, if you're sure I can't sell you any brushes—"

That brought the laugh he had hoped for.

"—I'll be getting along. I've two more calls here, then I'll get a cup of tea, and—"

"I could make you a cup of tea, if you like," the woman said, apparently not suspecting that he had given her the broad hint. "As a matter of fact, it's rather funny really. Mr. Kennedy doesn't like me buying anything from the door, and seeing how he makes his money that *is* a bit of a joke, isn't it?" She stood aside for Radlett to pass. "But as you work for him, I don't suppose he'll object. As a matter of fact you *could* just look out the brushes, I think we could do with some new ones." She led the way through a hallway and a passage into a modern kitchen; everything that Radlett could see had quality here, it was one of the apartments he had talked about to Roger. Most of the doors were open, and the garrulous woman seemed to be an efficient servant, everything was spick-and-span. "I'll leave you here and just finish off in the bedroom," she went on.

Radlett said: "It's very good of you. I—er—I—" he gave the impression that he was acutely embarrassed. "I wonder if you'd mind if I used the bathroom?"

"Oh, the lav!" She laughed again. "Help yourself, and you can find your way back when you're ready."

She did not watch him as he went out, found the bathroom, locked himself in, and waited until she passed the door. Then he slipped out and went into a long, narrow room overlooking Regent's Park, all brightly lit by the sun. He did not glance outside, but looked round swiftly, saw a table at one end of the room with a typewriter standing beside it. He stepped across. It was a small Smith Corona portable, not at all what he wanted. He looked quickly through the drawers of the desk, alert for any sound from the bedroom; he heard none. He went out, glanced into the small dining-room, and then heard the woman coming. He slipped into the bathroom again. She did not appear to notice that the door was ajar, but hurried to the kitchen where a whistling kettle began to pipe its summons. Radlett stepped out of the bathroom and into the bedroom; it was at the back, as long and narrow as the front room, and beautifully appointed.

There were twin beds, and a small dressing-room led off
one side. Radlett stepped towards this, saw a woman's
toilet accessories on the dressing-table in the dressing-
room, glanced further in—and saw a silver photograph
frame lying face downwards.

He went in, turned the photograph over, and saw
the smiling face of Brian Colson, who had killed the
newspaperman Anvill.

*   *   *   *   *

Roger said: "All right, Radlett, thanks a lot. Very
nice work. We'll check Kennedy's second wife; it looks
as if she was a Mrs. Colson. Have you been to Marlo's
place yet?"

"No."

"Make it the last on your list," Roger ordered.

*   *   *   *   *

Radlett wasn't too pleased by that instruction, but he
decided that it would be folly to disobey it. The quicker
he got the Marlo apartment done the better he would
like it, but West was always on the ball, and knew that
the other two would probably be done more quickly.

Widderman's apartment was in Knightsbridge,
Muriel Kennedy's in Kensington, both in the same
general direction. Radlett went to Widderman's first. A
small manservant opened the door to him, was politely
uninterested in brushes, and did not let Radlett set foot
in the apartment. Radlett felt uneasily aware of absolute
failure, but did not see what else he could have done.

He rode on his motor-scooter along Princes Gate, to
the small house near the Victoria and Albert Museum
where Muriel Kennedy had her flat. All he knew was
that it was a service flat on the third floor of the old
Georgian house, which had recently been painted and
decorated and had an atmosphere of old-world London.

He rang the bell, but there was no answer. He rang it
again, and then tapped lightly, but heard no sound

inside the flat. Now his heart was beginning to pound. In some ways this was the worst moment, the one which had made him make sure that West would support him if he were caught. It was one thing to be invited into a house or flat, another to force entry without a search warrant. He went to the head of the stairs and listened intently, but heard no sound. He took out a small toolkit, and went back to the front door of the apartment, worked on the lock for fully five minutes, then heard it click back.

His mouth was dry as he pushed the door open. It squeaked a little, but not enough to be heard downstairs. He pushed it wide enough to step through, went inside, and stood for a moment in a large room, overlooking the museums. Traffic was passing normally, and he saw two policemen on the other side of the road, talking. He looked into the other rooms in the flat—a medium-sized bedroom, a much smaller bedroom, bathroom and kitchen. The appointments were good without being luxurious. He looked about the main bedroom for a typewriter but did not see one, although again his attention was attracted by a photograph, not one lying on its face; it was on a table near the bed, a good portrait study of Roger West.

It was signed: *"With all love, Roger."*

*   *   *   *   *

"My God!" breathed Radlett. Then he thought: *But he sent me in here.*

Radlett opened the wardrobe door; all the clothes were women's. Hurrying, he went into the small bedroom, which had a single bed in the corner, and a built-in cupboard for a wardrobe; inside this were two suits, and he felt almost certain that they were West's size. In the chest-of-drawers there were men's good quality shirts and accessories; it looked as if West stayed here from time to time, and had an emergency wardrobe available.

Was Muriel his mistress?

If she was, why had West allowed him to come here?

Radlett moved quickly from the small bedroom back to the big living-room and lounge, and stood in the middle of it, looking about him, trying to get West out of his mind. There was no typing table, nothing to suggest that Muriel Kennedy brought work home with her. Then he saw a small oak gateleg table which stood very solid, and the leaf of which was hanging down. It hid a small portable typewriter in a beige-coloured case. Radlett squeezed between the table and the wall, and picked up the machine: it was an Olivetti. He unzipped the cover and placed the machine on the table, put in a sheet of writing paper, struck all the small letters, then all the capitals. Next he wrote the old typing school sentence in small letters and large:

The quick brown fox jumped over the lazy dog

THE QUICK BROWN FOX JUMPED OVER THE LAZY DOG

Finished, he folded the paper and put it carefully away in his wallet, then hunted for and found the serial number of the machine, and wrote that down. West would have to make sure that the Yard got hold of the machine quickly, but it had to be found here by someone with the right of entry; two officers with a search warrant, which could now be justified after the raid. He could leave the details to West. My God, couldn't he! He zipped the machine up in its container, excited with his success, put it back so that no one could tell that it had been moved, and then picked up the telephone. He dialled WHI 1212—that would be quicker than 999 to get hold of West in person. He heard the ringing sound, and it went on and on; he could never remember being kept waiting for so long. What the devil was the matter with the switchboard? What—

"New Scotland Yard."

"Give me Superintendent West, in a hurry," Radlett said. "Detective Sergeant Radlett here."

"Hold on, please." The operator seemed quite remote and uninterested. Radlett stood facing the door, with buzzing noises coming from the telephone and muted traffic noises from the closed window, making it impossible to be sure that there were no noises on the stairs. Why should there be? *Where was West?* What was his photograph doing—?

"Hallo, Radlett." West spoke as if there were no such thing as haste. "Where are you?"

"I'm at Muriel Kennedy's place. I've searched the flat thoroughly, and the typewriter's here," said Radlett. He paused for a reaction, but none came, so he went on hurriedly, "I've got some type specimens. There's no doubt about it being the machine we're after."

"*Very* nice work," West said, as if he meant it fervently. "There are two men in a Q car near the flat. I'll send them word by radio to watch it and pick up anyone who comes out with a typewriter, or a case which might hold a typewriter. You've done your job. Get out as quickly as you can."

"Thanks," said Radlett, hastily. "But, Mr. West, there's one thing—"

He heard West ring off, so it was too late to say anything about the photograph. He felt relieved at the thoroughness with which West had arranged all this, realised that he should have expected it, rang off, and paused long enough to light a cigarette. Then he shook his head. He took a last glance at the typewriter, and moved towards the front door; everything was over now, and he hoped he wouldn't have to tackle a job like this again for a long time.

He opened the landing door.

Two men, each wearing a cloth cap pulled low over his forehead and over the back of his head, stood there. Before he could speak, almost before the shock had hit

him, the taller of the two men kicked out, buried a foot
in his stomach, and pushed him back into the room. He
staggered against the door, tried to recover in time to
get a judo hold, then saw them leaping at him, and
knew he hadn't a chance.

22

ANXIETY

ROGER leaned forward at his desk, lifted the telephone
and called *Information*, and was answered before he
actually put his questions:

"No, Radlett hasn't been seen to come out of the
house, and there's still no trace of Muriel Kennedy.
She isn't at Widderman's office, but Widderman's still
there, and Kennedy and Marlo are at the *Zipp* offices."

"What about the Q car?"

"Still standing by."

Roger said: "Right, thanks," and rang off. Cope was
talking to a Divisional man about a smash and grab
which had been reported only a few minutes ago. Roger
scribbled a note: "I'm with Hardy," thrust it in front
of Cope's nose, and went out. On second thoughts, he
turned back to get his hat, and jammed it on the back
of his head as he walked along to Hardy's office. Hardy
was in, and alone; only the tiredness of his eyes hinted
at the strain under which he was living.

"Hallo, Handsome. What's on your mind?"

Roger told him.

Hardy said: "You never know what to expect next
in this case." The very moderation of his phrasing made
the comment sound more vehement. "Did Radlett say
the woman's flat was empty when he got there?"

"He said he'd searched thoroughly, and I shouldn't
think he'd miss anyone hiding."

"And the Q car men haven't seen anyone else go in back or front?"

"No."

"So someone was in one of the other apartments," Hardy said. "Have we any idea who?"

"No," said Roger.

"What do you want to do."

Roger said: "There's only one thing I can do. I sent Radlett to break in on my own authority, and didn't consult you or anyone else. He's got no right there, and whoever is behind this knows it. We can only get in, legally, on some pretext. If we take a chance and send an official search party to break in, we could really be in trouble."

Hardy was sitting back and looking at him almost blankly.

"We could get a warrant."

"Against Muriel Kennedy? With her father or some legal know-all sitting on our shoulders ready to throw the book at us? If we got one without being able to justify it by finding incriminating evidence, we'd start a squeal louder than the last one."

"What are you driving at, Handsome?" demanded Hardy, but the question was rhetorical; he knew.

"I've got to go and find Radlett."

"You'd have two books thrown at you," Hardy said.

Roger said: "The Press has already singled me out as the villain of the piece, with Birwitz a runner-up. If he and I run into trouble, we can always be suspended from duty, and if the worst comes to the worst we can be fired."

"Now, listen, Handsome—"

"Well, can't we?"

Hardy said: "I suppose you're right. But I don't like the idea of you—"

"I've told you so that if we do have to have a showdown, you'll know in advance what to expect," Roger said. "But officially, you don't know anything about it." After a pause, he went on: "There's one thing you can do."

"Name it."

"Have the four flats covered—all of those which Radlett visited or planned to visit. Have all our suspects followed wherever they go. Make sure there's a concentration of men in the Knightsbridge area in case I need emergency help."

"I'll do that," Hardy promised.

"Thanks." Roger flicked a finger towards the Assistant Commissioner, and went out. For a moment he stood outside the door, frowning, heart thumping. He felt exactly as Birwitz and Radlett must have done, although he had brought this on himself. They had been anxious for official backing—as he was—but Hardy had seemed almost tongue-tied. Hardy should have over-ruled him, should have insisted on signing a search warrant and making this official.

Why hadn't he?

Roger went slowly along to his own office, knowing how so many others had felt, knowing just how low morale had fallen at the Yard. The truth was that he had doubts of Hardy, and Hardy probably had doubts of him. When it was all over, if everything went smoothly, then he would laugh at himself for those doubts, he and Hardy would probably be much closer than they had ever been, but just now—Hardy was willing to let him stick his neck right out.

He looked into his own office.

"Hi, Handsome," Cope said. "Birwitz says can you spare him ten minutes. It's urgent."

"Where is he?"

"Down in the canteen. I said I'd call him."

"Tell him to meet me at my car," Roger said. "You're going to get some orders from Hardy before long; make sure everyone jumps to them."

"What's this?"

"You'll find out," Roger said.

It was nearly one o'clock when he reached his car, and one of the uniformed men on duty in the Yard came over briskly, to ask if he wanted a driver.

"I've one coming," Roger said. "Thanks." He saw Birwitz hurrying, his jaws working as if he was gulping food down. It was odd that a man who was so good on the tennis court should move so clumsily. Birwitz drew up. "Get in and take the wheel," ordered Roger. "You can tell me all about it on the way. We're heading for Knightsbridge."

"Knightsbridge!"

"Why not?"

Birwitz took the key, switched on the ignition, and eased the car towards the Embankment. He did not reply until he was safely out of the Yard, and Roger wondered how much of that was due to concentration, and how much was due to the fact that Birwitz was trying to make up his mind what to say.

Remember, Birwitz might not be reliable, either.

"My wife had another message," Birwitz said at last.

"What do they want now?"

After a momentary pause, Birwitz said: "You," and then trod on the accelerator so that he could beat the lights opposite Big Ben. They swung right, then left into Parliament Square. "I was told to send you to a house in Knightsbridge—and to persuade you that you ought to go there on your own."

Not *reliable*?

"When did this message come in?"

"Half an hour ago," answered Birwitz. "Betty Green's at a nursing home, and I was waiting there in case she came round and talked. Meg knew where to find me. She said the message was received at three minutes past twelve."

Ten minutes or so after Radlett had called, Roger realised; the other side was working very quickly. Against time?

Birwitz said: "Mr. West?"

"Yes."

"There are—there are two brush salesmen at my home at the moment. My wife telephoned under duress." Birwitz's lips were working. "One of the men spoke to me. He told me what would happen to my wife if I didn't obey them. If you don't turn up at that house on your own—"

He broke off. Roger saw how tight his hands were on the steering wheel, saw the whiteness of the knuckles. He seemed to drive mechanically, not too fast, never causing the slightest danger, and he spoke in a low-pitched but perfectly controlled voice, as if about ordinary, everyday things.

Roger said: "They don't miss much."

"They're devils," Birwitz said; he uttered the word in that low-pitched voice, without any particular emphasis. "If I go home until this is over, or if I send anyone to my bungalow, they say—"

"Yes?"

"They reminded me of what happened to Horace Green."

"I see," said Roger. "And this address? Is it Curlew Place?"

"How the devil do you know?" Birwitz's voice became shrill.

"Radlett's there," Roger said. He told Birwitz exactly what Radlett had told him, but said nothing about the Q cars and the other concentration of police which was being arranged. In an ironic way, he felt relieved. It was one thing to break into Muriel Kennedy's flat in order to make sure that the Yard, as an organisation, could not be damned. It was another thing to go there because of Birwitz's story; that made it wholly justifiable. There was just one factor that had to be remembered: that Birwitz might not be telling the truth. The story sounded true in every detail, it seemed to fit the circumstances, it was the kind of thing which the organisers of this campaign would do, but—he could be lying.

At this stage, did that matter?

Roger had to go in alone.

He said: "I'm going to force my way into that flat, and I don't know what to expect. I'm not going officially. I know now that they want me there very badly, and they want me on my own."

Birwitz said: "Not quite on your own."

"Meaning?"

"I was told to go there, after you."

"To do what?"

"Break into the top flat," Birwitz said. He raised a hand from the wheel and brought it down heavily on his knee. "What the hell are they trying to do?"

"Isolate us," Roger said.

"I don't follow you."

"You and I, as the scapegoats," Roger said, carefully. "And remember that a man with a very good mind, a police kind of mind, is behind all this."

"It's Kennedy all right."

"Sometimes I think it's too obvious that it's Kennedy," Roger said. "But who it is doesn't matter much at the moment. What they've got laid on is the important thing." He broke off suddenly and then ordered: "Pull in by that telephone kiosk over there. Double park."

Birwitz began: "Why do you—?" then stopped and carried out his instructions. Roger got out, went into the kiosk, and dialled Birwitz's own number. The ringing sound went on for a long time and when it stopped, a man answered.

Roger said: "This is Superintendent West. Is Mrs. Birwitz there, please?"

The man said: "I'm afraid she's gone out." After a pause he added: "Can I give her a message?"

"No," Roger said. "I'll call again."

"Right you are," the man said.

He might be a brush salesman, working under

instructions, but there was still no positive proof of Birwitz's story.

Roger went back to the car. Birwitz's forehead was filmed with sweat, and his hands were bunched.

"If anything happens to Meg—" he broke off. "My God, what a fool I was to start this."

"You didn't start it, remember," said Roger. "We're after the men or women who did, the men or women or the group of people who want to pour ridicule and contempt on the Yard, who want to get the Yard at sixes and sevens, so that—" he broke off.

"What?" Birwitz demanded.

Roger said: "No matter how you hated the Yard, would this be worth doing for revenge? Working on the nerves of police witnesses, causing emotional stresses, spreading doubt, scheming so that no policeman can look at the one he's working with and feel absolutely sure of him—would anyone do this for revenge? They might get at a man responsible for what happened to them, I can see Kennedy going all out to get Hardy, but not the whole of the Force. That doesn't make sense. Does it?"

"I suppose not," Birwitz said. "What does?"

"I think I know," Roger said softly. "I think it stands up." Birwitz snatched a glance at him, before taking a right turn. "A countrywide organisation of door-to-door salesmen, most of them genuine, a lot of them criminals. The police at sixes and sevens. A sudden swoop—not the odd burglary or the odd raid, but hundreds at a time, a whole series of robberies from private houses. If it was all done in one day, it would be more than the police could cope with. Nine out of ten of the criminals would get away with it, and as the loot would be in cash or in easily negotiable jewels, none of it worth more than a few hundred pounds, it would be easy to dispose of."

Birwitz said: "I suppose you could be right. But— it doesn't answer the big question."

"What question?"

"What are we going to do?"

Roger said: "We're going to break into that flat and find what it's all about—find out why they're so anxious to get you and me."

Birwitz said slowly: "You'll take the risk?"

"Can you see any way of avoiding it?"

"No," Birwitz agreed, and moistened his lips. "I can't. I thought you'd probably see a way." He concentrated on his driving for the next ten minutes, and then turned out into Old Brompton Road, showing that he knew London as well as Roger. "Now we won't be long," he said. "Have you any idea at all what to expect?"

"Just one thing," Roger said. "I expect them to lay on something which they think will fix me once and for all."

23

FORCED ENTRY

No one was loitering near Curlew Place, but across the road a radio van was parked without a driver; that was the original Q car. Two taxis at the front of a nearby cab rank always allowed the drivers behind them to take the fares; the first two were also Q cars. A removal van stood not far from the radio van, its flap down. Two men were sitting on furniture inside it, eating sandwiches and drinking tea out of enamel cups.

Traffic passed to and fro, unceasing.

Roger and Birwitz turned into the porch, tried the front door, and found it locked. Birwitz stood by the gate, Roger used a skeleton key, quickly, expertly; and the lock clicked back. He pushed the door open, and called: "All right." Birwitz came in and closed the door. The only light in the narrow hallway with the painted walls came from a fanlight and a landing window. There was no sound in the house.

Birwitz asked: "Who's going first?"

"You," Roger ordered, and the man from Richmond pushed past him and started up the stairs. They were carpeted, and footsteps made little sound. Birwitz paused to listen at the first landing, but soon went on. Roger followed, several stairs behind. The silence still lasted when they reached the top landing. Birwitz went straight to the door and stood with his back to Roger, working on the lock. Roger peered down the stairs. There was a click, the door sagged open, and Birwitz whispered:

"Okay."

As he spoke, there was a sound from downstairs. Roger swung round. He saw Rocky Marlo coming from the flat below, and behind Rocky were two men, one wearing a cloth cap, the other bare-headed, and looking bald—but in fact his head had been shaved, and his fair hair was just beginning to grow again. Marlo raised his hand and waved, and he came upstairs, grinning. The other men followed close behind.

"Go on in," Marlo said. "You invited yourself, Handsome, I'm told—go right in! You cops don't care what you do so long as you get the pickings, do you?"

Roger moved back, slowly.

"Birwitz can go in, too," said Marlo. "Go and join your little pal, Radlett. He's all right. He thought we were going to cut his throat, but we didn't—we had other ideas, didn't we, Handsome? Or wouldn't you know?"

Roger went into the small hall of the flat. The door of a long room opened, showing a small upright piano, the oak gateleg table, couches and easy chairs, and the drab walls of the museum, opposite.

"Nice little house-party," said Marlo. "Get a move on, Handsome, we haven't got all day. You're not saying much, are you? Didn't you expect a reception committee like this?"

"Whatever I expected, I got one," Roger said.

"And you're going to get a lot more you don't expect," said Marlo. He was just behind Roger, and gave him a push; not really rough, just enough to make him stagger into the long narrow room overlooking the park. Birwitz moved towards the window. Radlett was sitting in an armchair, with a patch of sticking plaster over his mouth, his grey eyes wide open and staring, his coat on back to front, so that it served as a strait jacket.

Marlo followed Roger into the room, and one of his men, the one whose head was shaved, came in with him; the other stayed outside, obviously on guard.

"So here we are, all friends together," Marlo sneered. "And I won't waste your time, Handsome, I'll put my proposition and then you can take it or leave it. I've got a big coup coming off. I've got over two hundred raids planned for tonight and they can't fail. The houses have all been properly cased, we know where the stuff is, it's a simple matter of going in and helping ourselves. We've got half of our salesmen ready for it, and we've got the selling laid on—it will all be small stuff, easier to sell than big stuff when it's hot. That clear, West?"

Roger said: "It's clear."

"Two hundred and eleven raids, as a matter of fact," said Marlo, and opened his mouth in a great guffaw of laughter. "You want to know why Green had to be killed? Because he knew what we were planning, he was one of the best casemen in the business. Know why Anvill had to go? Believe it or not, that newspaperman found out what we were planning. He came on it by accident, you needn't feel too sore about it. We couldn't leave him alive. As a matter of fact we thought *you* were on to it, that's why you had to be put away. But you were lucky, and when you came to the offices yesterday you proved that you'd fooled us into thinking you knew more than you did, Handsome—but you won't fool us again."

Roger didn't speak.

"So now you know the set-up." Marlo tossed back his head and gave another bellow of laughter. "Couldn't be tidier, could it? All we want now is someone who can make sure we can carry on nice and smoothly from now on. It's a perfect set-up, Handsome, the very best. Kennedy and me, we've worked it out perfectly. Now we've got you here at Muriel Kennedy's place, with a couple of your suits—one we stole when we raided a cleaner's near your home a few months ago, another we had copied. Remember that one you lost?"

Roger said: "I remember." But until this moment, he had not given the loss a thought for weeks.

"Well, it's all here," said Marlo. "And there's a pretty photograph of you on Muriel Kennedy's dressing-table, showing how close you two were. Radlett was quite shocked when he saw it, weren't you, Sarge?" Marlo glanced at the helpless man on the easy chair, then back at Roger; again he gave a bellow of laughter, a tell-tale sign that his nerves were stretched taut. "Okay, Handsome, you can take it which way you like. You can play it our way, just stringing along with us, and it will be worth twice as much dough as you get a month as a copper. Another five thou' a year, Handsome—how does that sound? And all you've got to do is lay off me and my boys whenever I give the word. I won't make it too obvious, I'll let you catch a boy now and again. I'm no fool. All I want is a nice easy life for me and the boys. That right, Deemer?"

The man at the door said: "That's right, Rocky."

"So you see how easy it is," said Marlo. "You come in with us, and we fix it so tight that you can't get out when you're in—we fix it by having Radlett's throat cut and framing you for it. In fact, Handsome, you're

framed already. You can play it our way, in which case
we'll see you through, or you can be a good, honest
copper, and you'll be strung up for killing Radlett, and
a lot of nasty personal details about your love life with
Muriel Kennedy will come out. It won't be any use
Muriel denying it, either, because your men will be
here before she can get rid of your clothes and the other
evidence that you've spent a lot of cosy little hours in
the love nest. What's it to be, Handsome? For us or
against us?"

"If it's for you," Roger said heavily, "how can you
guarantee that I won't get caught for Radlett's murder?"

"That's a good question, that shows what a wise guy
you are!" Marlo began to laugh again, but stopped
himself, as if he felt dangerously on edge, knowing
that this was the fateful moment. "Make up your mind,
Handsome. You can tell your old pal Hardy that you
got here and found Radlett dead. And you can say
you had information that he was in danger, that's why
you got in without a warrant. You'll be okay—for as
long as you do what I tell you. If you turn round on us
—okay, we'll have the photograph."

Roger echoed: "Photograph?"

"That's right," said Marlo. "The photograph—you
killing Radlett."

Roger caught his breath.

"What's the difference?" demanded Marlo. "He's
going to be put away, anyway. What's the difference
who kills him?" .

Roger glanced at Radlett, who was motionless; and
so helpless.

"Give our Mr. West the knife, Deemer," ordered
Marlo. "It's the one used to kill Green, Handsome,
isn't that a funny coincidence? One slash will be
enough. Got the camera for me, Deemer?"

Deemer said: "It's here okay, Rocky."

Roger saw a camera change hands; an ordinary 35

millimetre camera with a flash-light bulb attached. Marlo took it in both hands, put it to his eye, and made a clicking noise with his tongue as he focused on Radlett.

Roger said: "Birwitz—"

"You don't have to worry about our Witzy," said Marlo. "He's going to be one of our witnesses. If he doesn't do what he's told, his wife won't live to see the day out. Follow me, Handsome?" Marlo drew a step nearer, and his eyes narrowed, something of his hatred showed in them; but he did not come too close, not near enough for Roger to strike. "Get it straight, West. It's all or nothing. If I lose, okay, I lose. If I get strung up for capital murder, okay, I get strung up. We've all got to die. I'm gambling on you and Birwitz. I'm gambling on you wanting to save your lives and your reputations and your wives. Because if you don't play it my way, I'll see you both lose everything you've got. If you kill Radlett and I take a pretty picture—okay, that's absolutely okay. If you leave me to kill Radlett—"

Rocky broke off.

"You got to admit," said Deemer, "it's a clever idea. Ain't it, copper?"

24

CLEVER IDEA

"Yes," Roger agreed, "it's a clever idea." He looked at Marlo, who had backed away as if he were nervous of physical violence; and he glanced at Deemer in the doorway, then at Birwitz. Birwitz's face was like granite, and his lips were set so tightly they seemed to be just a thin line. Radlett shifted his position a little, and made a grunting noise. "Where does Widderman come in this?" Roger demanded.

"Nowhere, except to fool you," said Marlo. "We

fixed you in that lift at his place, to make sure you kept him in your sights, and incidentally to put you out of action for a day or two. The scare you got when you went down in that lift gave me a real big laugh."

Roger said stonily: "What about Widderman's secretary?"

"She's not in it, either," said Marlo. "That was part of the scheme, Handsome, to keep you looking in the wrong places. Kennedy's in it, but he couldn't help himself, poor guy. You want to know the truth about Kennedy? He never could keep his hands clean. When he was a copper he took bribes, wasn't that a terrible thing? And afterwards he was always letting his hands roam, that was Kennedy. He had to find some quick dough, and I found it for him—in return for a little help. He was invaluable after that, Kennedy was, and it got you looking three ways, too. And just to keep up the pressure, I fixed it so that his stepson was on my payroll. Guy named Colson, Brian Colson. It's a funny thing about Colson, he was always the boy for me. Birds of a feather, don't they say? Colson couldn't keep his hands off other people's money, either, so I put on a bit of a squeeze. It always works."

"Does it?" asked Roger, huskily.

"You're going to find out, Handsome! Just look at the position again. All you have to do as a copper is make it easy for me and the boys. You lay off my best men, and if there's a raid laid on for a night club, okay, you give me warning. You'll be my grapevine at Scotland Yard—like Kennedy, only more so. And if you ever feel like changing your mind, there'll be that photograph. Or you can play it like an honest copper, and you won't get out of this room a free man. I'll kill Radlett and get out. Birwitz is too fond of his wife to take any chances, he'll let us get away. Won't you, Witzy?"

The sweat stood out in beads on Birwitz's forehead.

Marlo snarled: "*Answer me, copper!*"

"I'll answer you," Birwitz said in a stony voice. It

was impossible to be sure what he was going to say, and agonising to wait for it. He seemed to pause for an age. "I wouldn't let you out of my sight for ten seconds, Marlo. I'm a policeman. Got that? I'm a copper, like West. I took your money and I gave you the information with West's knowledge, under his orders. That what you want to know?"

Marlo exclaimed: "That's a lie!"

"Rocky," Deemer said, "Witzy's forgotten that he's got a loving wife."

"I haven't forgotten anything," Birwitz grated. "There's a time when you have to stop pretending. I've stopped. And now I'm going to break your neck—"

"Keep away from me!" Marlo dodged back, tossed the camera into a chair, and snatched out a flick-knife; the click came sharply and viciously. Deemer snatched one from his pocket at the same time, tossed it in the air, catching it again so that he could fling it.

"Okay, Rocky?" He sounded quite calm.

"Let them have it," Marlo said savagely. "Let them—"

Birwitz flung himself at Deemer, as the knife came. Roger saw his body hide the knife, heard the little suck of sound as it went into his chest. At the same time, Marlo dodged to one side, but he couldn't get out of the way of Birwitz's flying arms, and Roger flung himself forward in a flying tackle, to grab his legs and bring him down.

He saw Deemer, with Birwitz's hands round his throat, head going to and fro like a ventriloquist's dummy, eyes rolling. He heard footsteps on the stairs as the other man ran. He saw Marlo trying to get a hold on his knife, and he got to his feet and stamped on the man's wrist, then kicked the knife away.

Then he went to the window, flung it up, and called: "Get a move on, you chaps!"

When the Q car men and the others, six in all,

rushed into the flat, Birwitz was sitting on the corner
of the table, pressing a hand against his chest, to stop
the bleeding, Roger was trying to help Radlett out of
his coat, Marlo was sitting against the wall, glaring,
and nursing his wrist, Deemer was lying in a corner,
unconscious, and the guard had run away into the
arms of police waiting outside. That was all.

* * * * *

"And it was as simple as that," Roger said to Hardy,
that afternoon. He was feeling wholly content since
hearing that Birwitz's wound was not serious; Birwitz
had been taken home from the casualty ward of St.
George's Hospital, and men from the Division had
gone to the rescue of his wife. "The kingpin was Marlo,
who had much more organising ability than I realized.
Kennedy began this chiefly out of revenge. He used
Marlo, who also hated us, and gradually it widened.
The revenge motive itself wasn't strong enough, but
when the widespread robberies were planned, everything was worthwhile. Kennedy never lost sight of his
own first objective—to make fools of us, to get us suspecting one another. There was no organisation among
lawyers—the lawyers simply cashed in, without knowing what gave them police-witnesses on one foot.
People like Mrs. Haughton were lucky, that was all—
lucky because the rot had started with police witnesses
against them. Kennedy used his brush-salesmen as a
cover, of course, most of them genuine, many of them
crooks who knew all the ropes, but instead of doing a
job or two at a time, he planned one big coup—at a
time when we wouldn't know whether we were on our
heads or our heels."

Hardy said: "He came very near splitting the Yard
wide open."

"He made a simple mistake," Roger pointed out.
"He thought that because Kennedy could be bought
and made to do what he wanted, a lot of others could.

Birwitz looked easy, after what he did because of his wife, and I—" Roger shrugged. "He thought I'd play if the money was big enough. It would have been easy for Birwitz and as easy for me—if we'd been made the way Kennedy is."

Hardy frowned.

"Kennedy's on a charge across at Cannon Row— you know that. Cope went to see the second wife, who's grief-stricken because her son is likely to hang as a murderer—she says she didn't know anything about Kennedy's under-cover work. Whether she did or not will come out sooner or later. Widderman has heard what has happened, too—and, incidentally, Kennedy had warned his daughter to stay out of town today. She took his advice. She swears she knew nothing about the use of the typewriter, but did know that Marlo had rented the flat under hers, furnished, for a few months. Have you heard about the condition of Betty Green?"

"Birwitz suggests she should go and stay with him and his wife for a week or two, and that's what she will probably do," said Roger. "Birwitz telephoned his wife and fixed it. He's applied for a transfer to the Yard, and I told him he could rely on it."

"He can," said Hardy, gruffly. "And you can rely on the strongest commendation I can give you. I've arranged with the Commissioner to release a detailed story of what happened at Knightsbridge, and a full release of the work you and Birwitz have done. I don't think you'll find any newspaper criticism for a while."

"I can do without any," Roger remarked drily.

"And there's something you can do with," said Hardy. "A couple of weeks off. That's an order, Handsome. If you want longer, that's all right with me."

He stood up, and held out his hand.

*　　*　　*　　*　　*

Roger saw Betty Green, at the Birwitzes' home, later that evening. She was pale and distressed, but had

regained a composure which promised well for her
future. Meg Birwitz tried to apologise for her doubts,
Roger refused to let her, and Birwitz saw him to the
car.

Janet was sitting at the wheel; she refused to let
Roger drive.

As she turned into Richmond High Street, she said:
"Home, darling?"

"Certainly not," said Roger. "We're going to the
West End, and I'm going to find out at first hand what
Widderman's shows are like. I'm told that one of his
clubs puts on a very good dinner. All right with you?"

"Why do you want to choose a Widderman club?"
demanded Janet suspiciously. "You promised me that
you wouldn't think or even talk about Yard business
for at least two weeks."

"Who wants to think or talk about cops and rob-
bers?" demanded Roger. "We're going to a Widderman place because he sent me a pass for any of his
shows and any of his clubs, good for two people, for as
often as I like to use it. There was a note with it."
Roger chuckled. " 'If you see anything which
resembles a disorderly house or which breaks the law, I
undertake to report in person to Scotland Yard the
following morning, for any action you care to take.' "

"Show me," ordered Janet, and when Roger took
the card out of his pocket she pulled into the side of the
road and read. Her eyes lit up.

"There's just one thing," she said.

"What's that?"

"Isn't this a kind of bribery and corruption? I mean,
going in without paying?'

"If it is," said Roger, "I'm corrupted. How about
getting a move on? I'm told that the first show at the
High-Lo starts at nine-thirty, we'll never get through
dinner in time if we don't hurry."

THE END